R. J. L

Realm of
THORNS

Gram-Co-Ink.

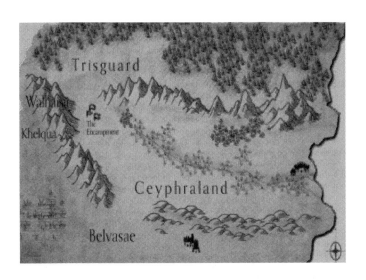

Trisguard

Wall...

Kheliqua

The Encampment

Ceyphraland

Belvasae

Books by R. J. Larson:

Books of the Infinite
Prophet
Judge
King
Realms of the Infinite
Exiles
Queen
DownFallen
Valor
Legends of the Forsaken Empire
Realm of Thorns (A novella)

Chapter 1

To whom can I speak and give warning? Who will listen to Me? My people refuse to hear; they turn away. The Eternal's Word offends them; they find no pleasure in it.

From *Books of the Prophets, The Rone'en*

Willing herself to appear serene, Eliyana of Khelqua watched her teachers.

Seated opposite her at the gold-inlaid amethyst table, the revered Torena's dark eyes glinted, fiercely at odds with her sedate wreath of silver-plaited hair, which gleamed beneath sheer formal veils. Her opponent, the smooth-shaven Kiyros—rotund as a subtly wrinkled tawny russet plum—waved her off dismissively.

Shaking his silver-curled head, he lectured Eliya. "Ignore her, Lady Eliyana. The revered Torena forgets that insecure victors rewrote history! I bless the heavens that she's alone in her solitary faith. Queen Cyphar and her consort, Gueron, instituted many social reforms that advanced our culture, yet they were unfairly maligned—their reputations besmirched by the ancient prophets and fanatics of Khelqua."

"Unfairly maligned?" Torena planted her long brown hands on the study table's shimmering surface. "Cyphar *murdered* all but one of her own grandsons and, according to the Sacred Word and Khelqua's official scribes, Gueron was a paid assassin. How was she fair?"

Kiyros' voice oozed contempt. "You're certain she wasn't? The 'Sacred Word', your treasured *Rone'en*, was written by those scribes and so-called prophets who scorned our Chaplet faith and brutally executed Cyphar and Gueron."

Torena exhaled, a woman controlling extraordinary impatience. "Were you there? No! We must rely on contemporary accounts. Ancient scribes and prophets recorded events independent of each other, which testifies to their veracity. Furthermore, your Chaplet faith

4

is nothing but Cyphar's self-serving pagan creed mixed with just enough of the Eternal's scriptures to make it inviting to Khelqua and the continent. The Chaplet goal is to obliterate our past! Yet, to deny and suppress the Rone'en is to scorn the faith that created and bound our Syvlande Empire."

"Faith?" Kiyros snorted. "Tyranny built and bound the empire. It deserves to crumble!"

Eliya gazed up at the palace study's carved stone roof-beams, then at a crack tracing it's way along the plastered walls from a recent quake. Once per week, her teachers contended with each other, their verbal battles so vociferous that one or both teachers should expire at every lesson from sheer exhaustion. Ironically, the following week, her teachers might argue the opposite opinions with equal ferocity, until she was convinced that Torena followed the Chaplet faith, and Kiyros harbored a dangerous devotion to the Eternal Liege—and that they'd thrash each other while defending their views. How could such behavior be proper while training a princess? She ought to scold them both. "Sir, and revered lady, I'm leaving."

Obviously not hearing her, Torena snapped at Kiyros, "If the empire falls, it will be because headstrong *spoiled* citizens rebel against common sense by calling laws tyranny, since too many citizens are reluctant to perform honest work! If you believe your life will be better after the empire falls, then you're deluding yourself."

"We will be free!"

Enough. Eliya tapped her fingertips on the glistening amethyst tabletop. If she reported half of her teachers' hot-headed utterances to her lord-father, they'd be imprisoned or worse. Particularly if Kiyros truly wanted the Empire to fall. Eliya abandoned her seat and shooed off Kiyros as if he were an errant bird. "Go then! Be free. And don't return. You're dismissed. Permanently."

Torena stood, her scholar's face calm. Mask-like. "Forgive me, Lady Eliya. I've forgotten—this was your last lesson."

Kiyros reddened visibly, then turned flustered. "Her last lesson? We're dismissed? And no one told me? Lady Eliya—"

"It's been kept secret." Not that she'd welcomed all the secrets. Eliya replaced her writing quills and inkstand in her silver carrying case, then closed its lid. "Don't worry, good sir, you'll be paid for the entire year's lessons as agreed."

"But ..." Kiyros hesitated. "What about the year's remaining lessons?"

Was he worried about lost prestige? Of no longer serving in her father's royal courts? Eliya smiled at him. "You're free, remember? Make arrangements with new students at your leisure. I'm being married off. Tomorrow morning, I leave for the northern realms as Trisguard's future queen."

"Well." Kiyros regathered some of his composure, then reached for his notes and reference scrolls. "That was sudden. The empire's northern realms, eh? Not surprising. I've heard rumors that Ceyphraland's rejected you, and that Belvasae's prince is in love with a commoner."

Though renowned for his discretion and keeping royal secrets, Kiyros delighted in sharing unflattering gossip he'd dredged from other citizens. Did he hope to enrage her? Eliya shrugged. "We've heard nothing from Belvasae or Ceyphraland. Whether the rumors you're spreading are true or not, my lord-father believes this northern alliance with Trisguard is Khelqua's best option. For, despite all its talk of leading the Syvlande Empire and possessing the imperial Sun Crown, Belvasae rarely manages its own lands competently. Unlike Khelqua and Trisguard. Farewell, Kiyros. I've enjoyed our debates."

His face scrunched like a drying, darkening plum, Kiyros swept up his writings and scribe-box and stalked out.

Torena watched him go, then spoke, her voice low and tranquil. "He's been a sometimes-worthy opponent."

Eliya studied her childhood mentor. "You seem content, revered lady, being newly-retired and no longer employed by the royal court."

"Oh, but I *am* employed, lady." Torena bowed her head, her sheer veils shimmering and drifting gently. Composed as a revered teacher should be, she gathered her scrolls and writing gear. "This morning, the king appointed me to escort the empire's only marriageable princess to Trisguard, then serve as your official attendant and scribe until you've acclimated to your new realm."

"Ah, there's another secret revealed." Eliya rested her parchments and wax note-tablet atop her writing box. "I should have known I wouldn't escape you, dear Torena. Not that I long to."

At least in Torena's company she'd have a perpetual reminder of home. As they walked through the glistening amethyst-and-gold halls of Khelqua's royal Ariym Palace, Torena asked, "What have you gleaned from enduring all our weekly debates with Kiyros?"

"That scholars can be stubborn and tiresome." Eliya shifted her writing gear, then teased her elder with a grin and a nudge. "And, that one teacher in particular can be trusted with an empire's secrets."

"Not the whole empire's worth," Torena protested. "I'd eventually be hunted and shot down by some Chaplet nobleman who's desperate to keep his own secrets to avoid paying for spiritual pardons. Don't worry, lady. I'll serve you only two years, and then retire. You'll be free to appoint your future companions from Trisguard's courtiers."

An unexpected pang nearly checked Eliya's footsteps. Only two years? She'd miss the revered lady. Just as she'd deeply miss her family and Khelqua. "Torena, I'll hate to leave Khelqua."

"Lady, Khelqua will hate to see you leave."

Before misty sentiment fogged Eliya's gaze completely, Torena added dryly, "The jewelers and fabric merchants will lose half their business the instant you step out of our lands."

If Torena had been one of her siblings, Eliya would have shoved her. Instead she laughed, then sobered. Tomorrow, she'd leave Ariym forever. Within days, she'd cross Khelqua's borders and never return. "I wish my departure could be delayed. What if my future husband's fanatically devoted to his Chaplet faith? What if he asks me to cease reading the Liege's words?"

"We pray and trust that the Eternal Liege will shelter you, lady." Hugging her treasured copy of the Rone'en closer, Torena added, "As for myself, I can't give up the Sacred Word, no matter what the cost. If reading it means that I'm sent onward from mortal life to the Eternal, I'll have no regrets."

Torena's composed, austere face, and her near-maternal grip on the Sacred Word, assured Eliya that she'd indeed give her life for her faith. Eliya shivered. Could she be as steadfast? "Don't plan your death. I need your courage. I know nothing of my future home. If Trisguard's Chaplet laws tighten, and my true beliefs are discovered and deemed traitorous ... even my royal blood won't save me."

They walked together, silent except for their sandaled feet clicking briskly against the corridor's amethyst and marble pavings. As they turned into the palace's main gold-and-amethyst corridor, Torena spoke, low and urgent, as if conveying a reluctant message. "Whatever your misgivings, lady, it's imperative that we leave as planned. I feel the Eternal urging us away from Ariym—from Khelqua itself. By the Liege's living Spirit, we must depart. Do you trust Him, Eliya?"

"More than I'd ever trust the Chaplet faith's revered Cyphar." Never mind that the legendary Cyphar's regal, golden-eyed image watched Eliya from every corner of Ariym's palace. Even now, the ancient queen's cutting gaze studied her unblinkingly from a quake-fractured mural framed within a wall's golden arcaded stones. Was Cyphar truly Eliya's ancestor? Perhaps. Eliya's eyes were the same clear gold. Her lord-father's eyes. The eyes of a lion sighting prey. Eternal spare her from ever becoming as merciless. Eliya hurried onward.

Keeping pace to her right, Torena exhaled. "If you mistrust the Eternal, then I've failed you and your lady-mother. Her most fervent wish was to see the Rone'en and the Eternal's faithful restored to Khelqua."

Suppressing weakening memories of her gentle, ever-devout mother, Eliya murmured, "No. Torena, you've not failed. And it's not that I don't trust the Eternal and His son, our Liege. Rather, it's my own family that's caused doubts. Their loyalties are so fleeting, that I question myself. Am I as flighty? Is my faith a fancy? I'd like to believe that it's not—that I'm capable of building a substantial and useful life, reflecting my faith. But then I look at ... others." Her lascivious lord-father, frivolous stepmother, and unreliable siblings, for example.

Could she trust any of them with her innermost secrets?

Torena shook her revered head. "How distressing. Such doubts from my most excellent student—the only one who never shirked lessons week after week."

"Your lessons were an escape from palatial boredom, revered lady, and they've given me a thirst for truth. Thank you. But now, the lessons have ended, and I've even more questions and concerns than I had when I first bowed to you as an apprentice-scribe."

"Your concerns are understandable, but I trust your abilities, Lady Eliya—and I've listened to many a noble-born who believes he or she could conquer the empire with less than half of your abilities. You will become invaluable to Trisguard."

Invaluable? To Trisguard's allied northern realms? Doubtful indeed, considering that she'd not received one hint of assurance from her future lord-king husband, Laros Rakiar of Trisguard, that she'd be truly welcomed.

Never mind the trinket-filled gold box his messenger had placed at her feet two weeks past, accompanied by Laros Rakiar's own note, filled with tributes to her beauty and accomplishments. Every exquisitely written word obviously paraphrased details he'd heard from some flattery-filled envoy.

Apparently, the lord-king of the northern realms didn't contemplate *her*, his future wife. She was a pretty formality. A trade agreement. A costly ornament to be stored away in dim apartments within his palace, unaccompanied by anyone from Khelqua except Torena and, perhaps, her personal maidservant, Vaiya. Her own friends, ladies, and even her relatives would be regarded as interfering interlopers within other royal courts. Father had emphasized this grievous detail more than once during Eliya's childhood. It didn't matter who married her—she must become a citizen of her wedded realm and not drag packs of 'foreigners' with her from Khelqua.

Yet she dreaded the isolation.

What if no one in Trisguard's court befriended her, or could be trusted? What if Laros Rakiar secretly scorned her? What if he never loved her as Father had loved her lamented late-mother? Worse, what if Trisguard's ruler was so strictly bound to the Chaplet faith that he ultimately persecuted her for trusting in the Eternal Liege?

To the Eternal, the Lord of all Sacred, she formed a silent prayer. "Defend me, I beg You! Protect me from my future enemies as I enter Trisguard."

Particularly if her most noble enemy should ever be her own husband.

His silence unnerved her.

✹

HER DARK CURLS TAMED and held back in a golden mesh caul, her rare purple robes in perfect order, Eliya knelt on the cold, smooth amethyst tiles before her father's gilded throne and her step-mother's honored bench, situated within arm's reach of the throne. "My lord-father ... I beg you ... let me stay in Khelqua one more week."

Her father, Rodiades, tetrarch of the empire's western realm of Khelqua, hid a yawn, smoothing his puffy face and silvering beard with one gnarled, ring-weighed hand. Sounding like a man longing for a nap, he grumbled, "Eliya, you've had the last nineteen years to visit your family and Khelqua. What use is one more week? Don't lose courage now—too much depends on your ability to captivate the northern realms. Trisguard's cavalcade is already traveling to meet you at their border, beyond the mountains."

What were her father's plans? Why did he need this alliance? She studied his bored visage and faded-gold eyes. If only she could read his mind. Or call upon insights from the Eternal, as prophets had done in the past. But—according to the Chaplet priests—the prophets were dead. And she was a mere princess whose royal father couldn't be bothered to speak her full name in a formal audience. Unless he thought Eliya *was* her full name.

Her stepmother, Amara—Rodiades' second wife, elevated from a league of royal darlings—leaned forward. "How I wish your royal mother had lived to see this day! She'd be so proud of your beauty—your dignified presence. Dear girl, believe me when I vow we'll miss you. But you must leave tomorrow as planned."

"Don't disgrace us with tears," her father urged. "Now ... your brothers and sister are in the courtyard, anticipating your farewell banquet. Don't keep them waiting."

He wouldn't attend? Eliya willed gentleness into her words. "My lord and father, because it is my last night, would you visit us later? After you've rested?"

"I cannot promise. I've letters to write to Belvasae and Ceyphraland tonight, announcing your marriage and formally inquiring as to why our correspondence is so sadly diminished. Not that I blame Belvasae and Ceyphraland for neglecting Khelqua. I've neglected them for Trisguard's concerns, and yours."

She bowed, then departed from the echoing amethyst throne room.

Willing herself to ignore the sting of tears.

⁂

IN THE ARCADE-FRAMED courtyard, Eliya smiled as her siblings cheered her arrival. The eldest, twenty-year-old Lord-prince Iscah, strode toward her, sun-bronzed and more vital than their father had been in years. Iscah held out his hands, drew Eliya near, and kissed her cheek. "You look sad. Don't brood, El. If you hate your husband, then I will gather an army and chase him from the northern realms."

His clear yellow-gold eyes sparkling with a seventeen-year-old's restless mischief, Eliya's second brother, Valo, joked, "I'm with Iscah. I say that Rakiar's gotten off too easily. He should wage an all-out battle for you. In fact, you're leaving months too early!" He waved at the courtyard's blooming fruit trees. "Spring is the time for war. *Summer's* end is the time for treaty brides."

Eliya swiped Valo's arm. "I forbid you and Iscah to attack my future husband. What if you defeat him? He'd hate me."

"Then we'd oust him and every other petty king from the empire and give Belvasae's sun-crown to Iscah."

A Khelqua prince wearing the emperor's sun crown. Such a marvelous feat hadn't been accomplished in three generations. Eliya smiled but shook her head. "You'd risk Khelqua."

"We'd guide the empire to its greatest glories." Iscah's lowered tone warned Eliya that he'd seriously considered the matter. "The Syvlande Empire is fading. Isn't this what the prophets warned? We must reunite the realms and strengthen our grip on the continent!"

Twelve-year-old Jesca, the youngest, and Eliya's only sister, laughed and edged into the middle of their conversation, her golden-brown eyes not as bright as Valo's or Eliya's, but afire with her love of schemes. "You should. We should! The empire would thank us, and future citizens would praise our names."

"If they don't kill us first." Valo goaded Jesca out of the circle, then followed her, calling over his shoulder, "Enough small talk! We've a feast to attend, and Eliya doesn't want to discuss warfare all night."

Just beyond the courtyard's entry to the palace, bells chimed, warning of approaching company—a dignitary they weren't permitted to ignore.

Iscah scowled at the entry, annoyance darkening his smooth-skinned bronze face. "Some highborn foreigner's intruding upon our feast."

Indeed. Eliya muted a sigh. Naturally, their last evening together would be consumed by formalities. Probably some finicky elder-diplomat from Belvasae's southern realms, who would complain about his difficult journey, bad food, and the fact that correspondence between the realms had dwindled to an insultingly meager level. Well, her lord-father could voice the same complaint against Belvasae and Ceyphraland. If either country dared to—

Her indignation froze as a tall, black-clad young man strode into the garden, his full mouth subtly pursed as if wary of the unexpected feast. Surveying Khelqua's royal siblings, his dark eyes gleamed. As he glanced at Eliya, he lifted one commanding eyebrow, countless unspoken thoughts hinting in his gaze. She held her breath, staring, listening as the servant called out, "Lord-king Danek of the Walhaisii."

Eliya blinked. Had the old Walhaisii lord-king died of his lingering illness earlier this year? Apparently so. Yet, no one had cared enough to mention it to her within her secluded court. But why should they? What was a minor upstart highland king compared to Khelqua's ancient lineage? Yet Lord-king Danek was certainly imposing. Even Iscah seemed impressed, his grim displeasure replaced by courtesy. Though Iscah's civility could just as easily be inspired by the fact that this Walhaisii king could undoubtedly throw him aside with a careless swat.

As Eliya stepped back, clearing a path toward the table, Jesca gripped her arm and whispered, "I'm so glad he's not your husband! *I want to marry him. I'll ask Father.*"

"Our lord-father would say you're too young." And giddy. Jesca's thoughts flitted from one idea to the next, her lively infatuations usually fading by sunset.

However, the Walhaisii lord-king provided plenty of reason for infatuation, from the sheen of his dark hair, to his understated, perfectly fitted gold-edged black robes, polished boots, and the wide leather belt emphasizing his warrior-worthy physique.

Iscah led Lord-king Danek to the feast. As they relaxed around the table, sharing soft bread, richly spiced simmered meats, dried fruit and cooled wine, the Walhaisii king said, "I'd no intention of barging into your feast uninvited, but the servants brought me here after sending word to your lord-father. He answered that he'd greet us later this evening. I owe him the Walhaisii's pledge of loyalty."

And a tribute, undoubtedly. Eliya swallowed her bread. Only the promise of some other king's rich gift would bring Khelqua's king out of hiding this evening. Even she had been unworthy of Father's notice. How unjust and—

No. She must not be angry with her lord-father when she departed in the morning. Rodiades had also obliquely insulted Lord-king Danek by not greeting him immediately. Above all, she must remind herself that her lord-father was even-handed in dispensing signs of arrogant indifference.

Impetuous as ever, Jesca smiled at the highlands' king. "My sister, Eliyana, has been ordered to leave tomorrow for the northern realms—Trisguard. Tetrarch Laros Rakiar's pledged to marry her. You should have spoken for her instead. Then we'd have her just beyond our borders."

As a stinging blush warmed her face, Eliya shook her head at Jesca. But Iscah grinned, and Valo joked to their guest, "What kept you from asking? Have stories of her bad temper reached you in the highlands?"

Lord-king Danek laughed, so good-natured with her teasing siblings that Eliya forgave Valo. Danek met Eliya's gaze, admiring her even as he jokingly quoted, "'The king of brambles and thorns said to the king of oaks, 'Give me your daughter that my son might marry her!' But the next morning the brambles were hacked to pieces and the thorns burned to ashes.'" Lowering his voice self-mockingly, Danek said, "I must preserve my realm, minor as it is."

Iscah lifted a gilded goblet of wine. "Are you saying the empire's remaining leaders would turn upon you? Don't you trust them?"

"The Syvlande's kings and lords haven't given me reason to mistrust them yet." Danek nodded at Iscah. "What's your opinion of the empire's future, Lord Iscah?"

Iscah's golden eyes shone over his goblet's gilded rim, and he paused before drinking. "The empire needs a strong ruler, not a league of quarrelsome kings."

"Or the empire needs to dissolve," Danek countered mildly. "Cooperation between the allied realms is breaking down—and if one tetrarch lord-king attempts to rule the others, we'll have open warfare from Khelqua's shores to the far beaches of eastern Ceyphraland."

Was Iscah going to choke on his ill-timed gulp of wine? Eliya watched her brother swallow hard, then set down his cup.

And, when Danek glanced away, Iscah's scowl toward their guest held promises of daggers.

❋

MASKING HIS DISDAIN, Danek swiped a fold of bread into his portion of tender spiced meat, then ate it. Agree to one all-powerful Syvlande emperor? Never. Marry a princess of Khelqua? Not in a fit of madness, much less cold sanity.

Clearly, the young Lord-prince Iscah fancied himself mature and capable of managing an empire. The Syvlande's remaining tetrarchs would wipe him out in a single battle, then hold a banquet over his grave—just before they turned upon each other.

As for marriage ... Danek pitied the sad, golden-eyed princess. Beauty notwithstanding, Lady Eliya was a mere game-piece for the allied northern realms. Their leader, Laros Rakiar, tetrarch of the north, undoubtedly envisioned himself as the next emperor. Only the Eternal could help the princess if she failed to bring the western realm's armies to his side.

And with this Iscah as her brother, she'd ultimately fail, for Iscah would obviously help no one's cause but his own.

Yet .... Danek mastered a frown. Was he being too harsh with these sheltered, inexperienced royal younglings? He *was* six years older. At their age, he'd also been overconfident. Convinced he could rule. Now, after governing the Walhaisii for only three months, his own mistrust, doubt, and cynicism darkened his judgments of others.

Nevertheless, Khelqua deserved scorn. The royal younglings' lord-father had betrayed the Eternal Liege twenty years past by bowing to adherents of the Chaplet faith, who'd clamored for the guiltless Liege's death. True, the Eternal Liege had returned to life among mortals—just long enough to prove He'd conquered death, but Khelqua's Tetrarch Rodiades *was* guilty of collusion and causing a wrongful death of the highest order.

How had Rodiades of the western realm failed to comprehend the Liege's significance—His Eternal Spirit within humble mortal form? All the Liege's miracles and the fulfilled prophecies had meant nothing to Rodiades. To preserve his own mortal wealth and power, Rodiades condemned an innocent man to die for teaching the truth of the ancient Word—the Rone'en. As a result, the Sacred Word was scorned and suppressed by factions devoted to the legendary figures of Cyphar and her consort, Gueron. Rodiades forced the Rone'en's believers from Khelqua.

Danek's family, sheltered in the highlands, had refused to enter Khelqua for years after the Liege's death, fearing persecution for their beliefs. Even at age five, Danek perceived his parents' turmoil. Refugees from Khelqua unfailingly arrived with fresh stories of imprisonment, torture and death, inflicted upon the Rone'en's believers by adherents of Cyphar's worldly Chaplet faith.

The charming pre-adolescent Princess Jesca beckoned Danek from his reverie. "Lord-king Danek, how long will you visit us?"

"Only for a short time, lady." Tonight only, if he dared to be rude. This palace, in fact all of Khelqua, set his flesh a-crawling with an agitation he couldn't explain. "I'm needed in the highlands."

"Your kingdom of thorns." Young Jesca's lighthearted laughter offset any offense.

As did the Princess Eliya's defensive rebuke. "Jesca! How can you be rude to our gracious guest?"

Still smiling, Jesca leaned toward Danek. "I apologize, my lord."

"No need, lady. I appreciate your concern." He included Eliya in his glance. She looked away. Toward the sound of distant calls and bells echoing from the palace corridors beyond the arcaded walls.

Prince Valo stood, his pale eyes brightening in his tawny face. "Our lord-father's visiting us after all."

Four guards entered the courtyard, unnerving Danek with their mask-like coldness as much as the swords and javelins they bore. A flicker of a story opened within his memories—accounts of an ancient queen-mother slaughtering her grandchildren. Danek stood, one hand relaxed alongside his gold-and-gem-decked courtly sword.

His hand twitched to draw the weapon as Rodiades himself entered the courtyard.

But not even the Eternal Liege would condone this proud tetrarch's murder. Danek subdued his loathing and bowed his head toward Rodiades. "Sire."

"Welcome, Walhaisii." Rodiades' golden eyes shone like old gilt in the afternoon sunlight. "How long will you stay?"

Or how soon could Khelqua be rid of him? Danek smiled. "I've come to pledge loyalty to you and pay tribute, though I can't delay—I'm needed in the highlands, and I'm in mourning for my lord-father. Apart from my tribute, I won't bring much joy to your courts."

"Understandable." Rodiades eased himself into Prince Valo's empty chair. "My condolences for your father's death."

"Thank you, sire. As for the length of my stay ... if you wish, as a favor to Khelqua and Trisguard both, I'll pay tribute and pledge loyalty tonight, then depart in the morning to lead your daughter's cavalcade safely through the highlands."

He almost regretted the offer the instant he voiced it. He'd be weeks guiding the sad princess from her home toward a realm that might not appreciate her, and this marriage was an imperial matter he'd no sane reason to take on. Rodiades grinned, genuine warmth turning his tired gaze from worn gilding to shimmering gold. "Thank you, my lord. I'll remember your kindness and repay you in the future."

Danek bowed his head toward Rodiades. Good deeds too often provoked unfortunate rewards.

Why had he offered?

Nevertheless, he'd keep his word—particularly if it meant leaving this quake-cracked old palace and Khelqua's scheming king.

Chapter 2

Morning sunlight warmed Eliya's face as she rode on horseback through Ariym's streets for the last time, watching as the capitol's citizens lifted their hands toward her lord-father, who rode ahead, leading Eliya away from home.

The revered Torena, and Eliya's maidservant, Vaiya, followed her on horseback, their veils floating in the gentle air, their garments glittering with beaded embroideries. Behind them lumbered a string of supply carts, all laden for her journey. Including the sumptuously gilded and cushioned violet wagon, built to shelter her in luxury from all storms as she traveled. But such luxuries wouldn't shelter her for long if Trisguard's lord-king and citizens despised her.

She must try to focus on this final farewell to Ariym. On this glorious morning, tinged with salt-breezes from the ocean in the distance.

Though the breezes didn't dispel the incense clouds from each street corner where the faithful were paying silver to the Chaplet priests, whose blessings preserved their souls from condemnation before the Eternal.

Yet even the faithful turned from their prayers beneath the priests' hands to gaze up at her in wonderment.

Eliya's violet and gold robes, her tiara, veils, and magnificently caparisoned horse—draped with cloth of gold and rich tassels—informed all of Ariym that this was no ordinary procession.

Merchants hailed her and citizens whistled and waved farewell as she rode past.

She waved and smiled now and then, but why mask her sorrow? Most likely, she'd never see Ariym and its citizens again.

Her grief increased as she rode after her lord-father along Ariym's largest and most stately stone bridge across the River Tynm. As soon as her entire cavalcade had crossed the bridge departing from Ariym, Rodiades dismounted and motioned Eliya down from her horse.

She mustn't cry. Her lord-father was smiling, and she'd shame him with tears.

He opened his gold-draped arms and lifted his hands as Eliya approached. "Here we part—my beautiful treasure." He kissed her forehead. "May Trisguard love you as richly as you deserve, and may you be crowned with honor!" Lowering his voice, he whispered, "Don't be afraid! Except for its lack of an ocean and its overabundance of trees and cold air, Trisguard's cities are the very image of Ariym in magnificence and spirit."

Exactly as she'd feared. Cities full of incense-burning Chaplet faithful, who'd turn against her the instant they realized she'd abandoned Chaplet ways for the Liege. She managed a smile for her lord-father, then kissed his whiskered cheek. "Thank you, my lord, for everything! I pray to deserve your trust and love."

Did she fancy he blinked down a few tears? If the tears were genuine, they vanished swiftly as Rodiades handed her over to his designated representative of Khelqua—Valo.

Rodiades lifted his chin at Valo, then pressed his ring-decked hands on Valo's shoulders. "Remember our conversation. Guard your sister and note everything you see in Trisguard, however unimportant. I want to breathe the very scent of northern air as I read your letters."

He kissed them both, then offered a smiling nod to the somber Lord-king Danek of the Walhaisii before riding away.

Immediately, Valo took charge. "Hurry. Let's leave the river valley and ride up to the Jizni Plains before the humidity suffocates us. If I have my way, we'll be in the mountains within three days."

Eliya scowled at him. "Don't rush me."

"Don't worry. I will."

*

ELIYA INHALED THE SCENT of the cedars bordering the sloping, sun-warmed clearing. How kind of Lord-king Danek to halt their journey early this evening at Walhaisii realm's border, so that tomorrow morning, she'd catch a final glimpse of Khelqua from the highland's foothills.

She turned from her view of the Jizni Plains and Khelqua's endless green river valley, then studied the lord-king's profile as he stood a short distance away, talking to several of his men. The Walhaisii lord-king needed no crown or golden robes to proclaim his authority—his men obviously respected him. Not to mention that he was splendid to behold.

If only he could be Laros Rakiar.

Valo stepped in front of Eliya, blocking her view. "Look away from him, sister. Doesn't your admiration belong only to your husband?"

He was serious. By all Creation, her usually charming and flirtatious younger brother was turning old and judgmental before her eyes. Eliya muttered, "I can admire whomever I please, yet remain faithful to my husband! In fact, I was just thinking of Rakiar. I pray he's a good man. Now, leave me alone."

Valo opened his mouth to argue. Until the world shivered beneath their feet.

The tremors increased, their ferocity swaying the magnificent cedars around the small meadow—shaking Eliya until she rocked backward.

Danek rushed toward them, grabbed Eliya's arm, and bellowed at Valo. "Center of the clearing! Everyone to the center of the clearing!"

Eliya tottered beneath the king's grip, then found her footing and ran with him to the center of the clearing.

Every member of her household and official cavalcade followed.

At the clearing's sloping edge where she'd been standing, cedars groaned and fell down the crumbling hillside. Far below, the vast river valley heaved, then opened like a rotting wineskin bursting at its seams, unleashing torrents of red-ochre waters from rifts torn into the land.

※

BATHED IN THE SUNSET'S crimson rays, accompanied by Lord-king Danek, Valo stood as near as he dared to the slope's crumbling edge. In silence, they stared down the devastated hillside into Khelqua's vast river valley below. Muddied red waters continued to spread from the fractured lands. Would the torrents fill the whole river valley? That staggering quake was the worst he'd ever experienced, and they'd suffered many in Ariym.

Had this quake shaken Ariym as badly as the flooding valley below? Undoubtedly his family was safe—

A light hand pressed his arm. Eliya halted beside him, gazing at the destruction below, her beautiful clean-cut profile tinged red in the sunlight. When she finally spoke, his sister's voice emerged half-choked, raw with grief for the quake's victims. "We were down there just a few hours ago! I hope the destruction and deaths aren't as extensive as they appear."

Just a few hours ago .... Valo drew in a quick breath. "If we hadn't hurried, we'd have been down there. Possibly swept away in those waters."

Still staring at the devastated valley, Eliya pressed her hands to her face and whispered through her fingers, "I pray our family's well. We'll send a messenger to Ariym tomorrow morning and ...."

Her words faded. She frowned, staring intently at the far horizon. "Look at that odd cloud forming along the skyline."

Valo studied the sweeping cloud-haze that hugged the horizon, its distance making him squint. Above the vast cloud-bank, the sky remained ruddy and clear. "Eliya, that's no cloud."

From behind them, Danek exhaled, his verdict weighed with intense concern. "That's water."

Eliya shook her head. "Impossible. Not covering that much of the horizon. It's a fog bank."

Another tremor shook the slope. Eliya tugged Valo away from the incline. When the tremor eased, she looked back at the smudged horizon. "It *must* be a fog bank."

No. Valo stared hard. The supposed fog darkened, enfolding the land as it stole along the horizon. If only Eliya could be right, but he couldn't blame her for preferring to misunderstand what she saw.

Silent, standing with Danek and Eliya, Valo watched Khelqua's horizon vanish beneath the sunset.

✻

DANEK MUTED HIS BREATH, and his inward horror. An onslaught of waters threatened Khelqua's very existence as he watched. Was this the fulfillment of the Eternal Liege's prophesied warning before His death?

Danek closed his eyes and prayed for the devastated realm below.

✻

ANOTHER PRE-DAWN QUAKE shivered through the clearing, jolting Eliya from a bleary-eyed doze in front of the open campfire. Beside her, wide awake, Revered Torena whispered prayers beneath her breath and clutched her most cherished possession—a copy of the Rone'en.

If any of Lord-king Danek's followers were Chaplet fanatics and recognized Torena's prayers to her Beloved Liege, they'd ridicule Torena at the very least—or persecute her openly if Danek approved. Thankfully, Torena's copy of the Sacred Words was covered in plain, unmarked leather, and her prayers remained whispered.

Eliya looked away from her revered-lady teacher. After witnessing last night's devastation in the river valley below, her own soul skittered between prayers on behalf of Khelqua, and silent inward pleas toward the Eternal. "Why?"

Beside her, Torena straightened. "What did you ask, Lady Eliya?"

"Nothing." Eliya stood and inhaled. Salt air tinged a hushed, pre-dawn breeze. Ocean air. Impossible. Her sleep-deprived senses were playing tricks on her.

Even so, she must see how Khelqua's vast river-valley realm had fared throughout the night. Had the waters ebbed?

She stood, eased her aching back and cramped legs, then walked down to the sloping western edge of the clearing. Valo joined her, silent as they stood and waited, inhaling sharp-humid air, and watching the day's first light touch the realm of Khelqua below.

At last, an ocean's endless vista met her gaze, avowing nothing but drowned life beneath its dark, rippling surface. Agony halted the breath in Eliya's lungs as she stared. She must still be asleep, caught in some appalling nightmare from which she'd wake.

Khelqua lay beneath a death-shadowed sea. In the dawn-lit skies above, far-flung hordes of scavenger-birds circled and glided over the dark waters, then dove toward the first reflections off the endless waves, feasting on the ocean-borne plunder of death.

Beside Eliya, Valo exhaled a low noise of mourning, and Torena began to sob. Eliya collapsed onto the quake-loosened soil and wailed.

❋

DANEK STOOD GUARD OVER the royal siblings as they mourned with their household and cavalcade of servants. If that ocean of dead waters ever drained, no sane person would resettle Khelqua's river valley. The prophesied reckoning had washed away everything. Had the Royal house of Khelqua and Ariym also been crushed and drowned beneath the foretold destruction of its vast river valley? Did Khelqua's ancient lineage now rest upon the two homeless royal younglings?

Princess Eliya's revered teacher stood and wiped her face, her expression bleak. She approached Danek and murmured, "This was foretold by the Liege, but how I prayed I wouldn't live to see it!"

"Agreed." Danek took refuge in silence. The morning skies brightened—an appalling contrast to the waters below. Every small village and fine city they'd passed in three days of travel through Khelqua was gone. Citizens, crops, cattle ... all gone.

If he squinted, Danek caught hints of faraway spires in the ocean. Sailing across those waters would be treacherous. When he could no longer endure the sight, Danek motioned two of his watching guardsmen forward. He'd send them to request volunteers and boats from his people.

A rescue expedition might console the Lady Eliya and young Valo.

❋

SEATED BEFORE THE CAMP'S cook-fire, Eliya covered her swollen eyes with her cold hands. The quakes and flood weren't real. She was delusional. Better to be insane than admit such a disaster had happened.

Nonetheless, when she opened her eyes, smears of dirt and grass offered evidence that she'd knelt and mourned her country's destruction. Khelqua's citizens and cities were swept away. Her family ... Iscah ... Jesca ... No. They were safe.

Ariym, just beyond the horizon, built upon high stone foundations, was undoubtedly safe, dry, though shaken by the quakes. She swiped at a grass-stain on her gown. "We'll send an envoy to the northern realms to tell Lord-king Laros what's happened, and that I'll be delayed."

"No." Valo, seated to her left, shook his head, his red-rimmed eyes remarkably stern. "You must honor the contract and arrive as pledged. Our lord-father gave his word."

Must? She glared at him. "But *you're* returning home."

"As soon as I find out what's happened, I'll catch up with you," he promised. "We'll both go mad, not knowing the extent of the disaster. If the whole river valley's an ocean ..."

His voice trailed off, sinking with their mutual unspoken fear. If the whole river valley was now an ocean, how could Ariym have escaped? She and Valo deluded themselves thinking otherwise.

Eliya rubbed fresh tears from her eyes. She blinked to clear her vision, and saw the Walhaisii lord-king approaching, his riding boots mud-smeared, his strong features grim. He nodded sympathetically to Eliya, then crouched near Valo, speaking to them both. "My men and I believe that if some of your servants ride north without venturing into the valley, they'll have a view of the lands east of Ariym within two days. Unless the Walhaisiis' lower valleys are also flooded."

Eliya straightened. "If the lower valleys are flooded, then they'll be delayed for considerably longer."

"It's possible," Danek admitted. "But I'd venture a guess that your lord-father would insist that you and Lord Valo continue your journey as planned. Why risk your lives in possible rapids or floods in the lower slopes? Your servants and my men are as concerned as we are, and they won't waste time while bringing us news in the north."

"Us?" Valo's dark eyebrows lifted. "Do you intend to accompany us, Lord-king Danek?"

"Yes. You'll lose a significant number of guardsmen on the scouting mission to the north, therefore my men and I will accompany you to the prearranged meeting place. Once you've met up with the northern tetrarch, we'll part ways. Until then, I'll ensure your safety."

Eliya nodded. "Thank you, sir."

He inclined his head slightly, then strode off to rejoin his men, his self-assurance and concern calming her distress. Valo cleared his throat. When Eliya glanced at him, he grumbled quietly, "It's for the best that I'm not going on the foray to Ariym. The way you've been watching him, as he watches you, Khelqua might have faced a terrible scandal."

Eliya shoved her brother. "Don't be insulting!"

He gripped her hand, forcing her to listen. "My perceptions of your behavior aren't insulting—they're what anyone else might believe as well. You know how people talk of the least things we do or say. I'm going to tell Torena to not let you out of her sight."

"She hasn't. Not even now." Eliya lifted her chin toward their revered teacher, who stood a discreet distance away, red-eyed as every Khelqua attendant in the camp. Torena noted their subdued squabble and pursed her lips disapprovingly. Eliya said, "You're perceiving what's not there, brother, so don't create a scandal by acting as if one exists. Let's save our thoughts and hearts for Khelqua. I pray our men return with good news."

She held Valo's gaze. They'd always been close—always maintained their relationship as equals, whether plotting mischief or enduring politics and ceremonies. When had he become so dictatorial? Didn't he realize that they might have no other family to depend upon? He must believe her. And trust her. Meanwhile, unless courtesy demanded it, she wouldn't risk even a glance at the Walhaisii lord-king. Perhaps, since Valo was so concerned about her behavior, she should hound him instead. "What are you planning to do?"

His forbidding expression remained, but a light grimace crossed his face, making him appear younger than seventeen. "I'll be checking my gear. Preparing to depart. You?"

"My gear's ready. I'll wait with Torena." She approached her teacher, who'd remained watchful, the Rone'en in her arms. Eliya nodded a greeting. "Revered lady, how are you?"

Torena's calm, self-certain voice quavered, and tears misted her eyes. "I'm praying, lady. Thank you for asking. Despite the prophecies, I can't believe what's happened. To see Khelqua flooded ... buried beneath a sea ..."

Eliya motioned her teacher to sit with her on a small mat near the fire. When they'd settled, Eliya leaned toward her and murmured, "You mentioned the prophecies. You warned me before we left Ariym that you felt compelled to hurry—to leave Ariym, and Khelqua itself. You suspected this disaster would occur, didn't you?"

Torena sniffled, then exhaled. "I feared it. Ariym's been suffering those quakes. Ancient plaster and murals that survived for hundreds upon hundreds of years in the palace were suddenly showing cracks and needing repairs ..."

Deliberately gentle-voiced, Ela said, "Yet you didn't warn my lord-father?"

Her revered-lady teacher straightened. "What could I say to him, lady? Your royal mother—I thank the Eternal for her!—appointed me to teach her children, because she believed the Eternal's prophecies. But your lord-father loathed the implied weakness of any faith. No. Lord-king Rodiades wouldn't listen to me about His prophecies. Much less, the Eternal's forgiveness. After all ... he signed the order for the Immortal Liege to die beneath a shaming chaplet of thorns."

True. Eliya stared up at the morning skies, her throat aching. Father had tolerated Mother's faith because he'd loved her. Yet, if Khelqua's ruin fulfilled the Liege's prophecies, shouldn't she trust Him completely? Only the Eternal could foretell such a disaster so accurately.

Eliya stood, hugging herself. "Thank you, Torena."

As the remnants of her divided cavalcade gathered its goods and supplies, she walked toward the crumbling hillside, edging around the upturned roots of fallen trees. Damp-soil scents met her nostrils before she reached the edge. A sickening miasma of humidity and sun-warmed death set her stomach churning, and in the skies above, giant golden birds circled, hovering over the relentless waters. Golden, glorious birds ... aeryons stooping downward toward the waves like common gulls ... to scavenge carcasses for their morning meal.

Carcasses washed forth from Khelqua's destruction.

Eliya pressed one sweat-dampened hand over her face, held the other to her stomach, and hurried toward the encampment, passing Lord-king Danek, who'd obviously followed to urge her away from the edge.

Even if her family survived, too many had died. She must convey her grief.

Before her maidservant, Vaiya, or Torena could help her, Eliya unpinned her hair, removed her embroidered purple cloak and bright blue over-gown, then unstrapped her second-best clothing chest and removed her prerequisite mourning clothes.

The black gown, she managed well enough. But the formal mourning cloak ... Tears blurred Eliya's vision as she struggled with the pins. Vaiya approached, cautiously lifted the tarnished silver pins from Eliya's hands and then fastened the cloak. Finished, Vaiya spoke, her timid voice congested. "Shall we all wear mourning, lady?"

"Yes. Thank you, Vaiya. Please tell the others."

Gripping the edges of her cloak, Eliya walked around the carts to rejoin Torena, seated near the ornate wagon. One of the chief guardsmen stood over the revered teacher, his low, harsh words sounding suspiciously foul. He bent and grasped Torena's opened book and all but shook it from her grasp. "...and you've been teaching *this* to her? To her brothers who're to rule us? This wretched history book's dividing our country and smearing our Chaplet faith!"

Torena faced him, strictly composed. "You misunderstand my role in the royal household. I've been—"

"Lying!" the man argued. "That's what your sort does! That's why we banished you all from Khelqua!"

"Enough!" Eliya stepped between them. "While we're grieving for Khelqua's loss, you're picking quarrels with an esteemed teacher!"

Valo hurried to intercede. "Aretes! Control yourself and return the book to the revered Lady Torena!"

His brown skin rage-reddened, Aretes argued, "With all respect, my lord, why should she be revered for teaching you lies?"

While Torena removed her cherished book from Aretes' grip, Eliya fixed her gaze on the infuriated Aretes. "You presume to know everything Lord-prince Valo and I've learned and believe. You overstep! Return to your duties and pray for your country. We're resuming our journey."

Aretes bowed, but his voice remained terse. "Forgive me. Lady. I was overcome. Those 'sacred' words of hers have destroyed Khelqua's peace—even the empire's peace! Every man and woman possessing that book place themselves above the Chaplet religious and their betters, provoking rebellion against our faith. They'll start a war that my men and I must finish."

Valo snarled, "You're still overcome if you're addressing us so disrespectfully and ignoring orders. Return to your men!"

The guardsman backed away, then pivoted on his booted heel to rejoin his watching men. But he complained to the air as he walked away—allowing everyone to hear. "We've been guarding a word-twisting, Rone'en cultist!"

Lord-king Danek and his men stepped into Aretes intended path. When Aretes started to protest, Danek bellowed, "Silence!"

The roared command echoed through the clearing. Aretes hushed. The Walhaisii lord-king didn't lower his powerful voice. Instead, he articulated each syllable for the entire encampment to hear. "The journey ahead is too difficult to waste time quarreling! We will have peace among us, and do not forget that you are all in *my* realm! I rule here! And I will have order!"

His strong features tensed, he strode to consult with Eliya and Valo. To them alone, he muttered, "That man remains insubordinate. You cannot allow him to travel with us unless he's punished."

Valo scowled, obviously feeling himself rebuked. Eliya rested a calming hand on her younger brother's shoulder, then faced Danek. "As you've declared, we're now in your realm. What punishment do you suggest?"

"Strip him of his rank. Put him in plain clothes, and make him walk on foot behind the lowest ranks. Whether his emotions are affected by the recent tragedy or not, who is he to insult one of Khelqua's revered teachers, much less argue with two of Khelqua's royal family? Remind him of his place. If he disagrees, he can leave us and return to Khelqua alone."

If Khelqua still existed. Pushing aside the thought, Eliya glanced up at her brother. "Father would have ordered him beaten and imprisoned, then cast out of service—I've seen him handle similar situations. But this decision is yours."

Valo's scowl faded, replaced by brooding uncertainty. After a long instant, he nodded at Danek. "I'll speak to Aretes first and remind him of what my lord-father would have done. This one time, I'll be merciful. As you say, we're in your realm."

Ordering punishments was easy. But watching the punishment effected ... that was a different matter. Eliya held her breath while Aretes stared past her, Valo, and Lord-king Danek as if they didn't exist.

As Valo pronounced Arete's punishment, the commander's face turned mask-like. Emotionless, he set aside his gleaming warrior's helm, stripped off his golden cloak with its purple insignias of rank, and then his weapons, armor, and official tunic.

As his former men gathered his discarded gear, Aretes bowed, then marched toward the lowest ranks of Eliya's cavalcade, scar-marked and powerful, his stride and bearing proclaiming his pride and unrepentant fury at guarding 'Rone'en cultists'. Unarmed, the man remained a threat.

Eliya swallowed her fears and motioned the silent Torena and their attendants to join the cavalcade and depart.

Valo rode beside her as they set out—neither of them risking a final weakening glance at Khelqua's distant, drowned horizon.

✳

THE NEXT MORNING, VALO greeted her the instant she stepped out of her tent, into the rugged, tree-edged clearing. "That renegade, Aretes, stole his gear and horse, then escaped last night."

Eliya studied her brother's somber face. Had he been brooding over Aretes—the first man he'd ever ordered punished? Well, she supposed she'd worry just as much. The man was a potential agitator. "Should we say, 'good riddance' or send a hunting party?"

"I sent men to track him at dawn. His trail headed north—toward Khelqua. They believe he intends to join the men we sent to Ariym."

"Don't worry." Eliya hugged his arm as they turned together toward the camp's central fire. "Most likely, we're free of him. But if he returns to create trouble, we'll deal with him."

Valo covered her hand with his own and gusted out a half-rueful, half-amused breath. "I'm supposed to be guarding you—protecting you—and you're having to reassure me."

"Yes, Father would be appalled."

"The morning we left, he called me to his chamber, blessed me, then told me to guard you with my life. Then again, when we parted. Obviously, he was worried."

"As if I can't be trusted."

"As if you're his favorite child. You know it's true."

"I knew no such thing!" However ... She hesitated. "It would be just like Father to hide a truth."

"It would," Valo admitted. "Be that as it may ... you had his favor. But I received the blessing."

The paternal blessing. Torena would see significance in that. Younger sons who received the paternal blessing were traditionally favored by the Eternal to lead the family. Did Father remember that little custom? Or had he deliberately disregarded Iscah as his heir? Eliya gripped Valo's arm again. "He burdened you, indeed."

What if Father and her family were dead? What if she and Valo were the only survivors? If so—

She cut off the dangerous thought and walked with her brother toward the fire and their morning meal.

❋

SHIFTING IN HER SADDLE, Eliya studied the setting sun over her shoulder, then stretched as much as she dared. Five days since the calamity, and she was silly enough to hope that the scouting party would return with good news of Ariym.

Undoubtedly, she was being overly optimistic. Schooling patience into her thoughts, she turned, adjusted her wearied horse's reins, then gazed ahead. Lord-king Danek had pledged that they'd spend the night in the open plain ahead—at the end of Walhaisii lands, and the beginning of Ceyphraland.

Would she ever visit Ceyphraland with her lord-husband? Perhaps.

She'd rather return to Khelqua.

She'd rather ....

Ahead of her the lead riders lifted their hands, slowing their pace. What could impede them on this plain? As Eliya eyed the lands ahead, Valo and their guards closed ranks around her, and Torena who rode behind her. Why were the guards so tense and silent?

Amid the deepening afternoon light, a peculiar and hushed sight met her gaze. An obviously wealthy cavalcade of gilded wagons and carts very much like her own.

A lifeless cavalcade.

No horses. No evening fires.

Only arrow-and-javelin-spiked bodies—dignitaries and soldiers cruelly massacred.

Chapter 3

His stomach knotting, Danek studied the carnage. Bodies, swollen and death-distorted, sprawled upon the ground before the cavalcade. Others slumped over the edges of carts, and in their seats—shot through before they'd ever suspected an attack.

What an appalling waste of life. Some forty guards and merchants or dignitaries lay here, many clad in Ceyphraland's conspicuous red and gold royal colors—obviously official emissaries heading toward Khelqua. Whose army had murdered these unsuspecting people?

Danek approached the ghostly cavalcade of carts and chariots, and wrenched an arrow from one of the bodies. Sun-burnished red wood gleamed at him. Yew from the Na'Khesh Mountains, north and east of here. Not the darker violet-brown tones of good Walhaisii yew.

Footsteps approached, light and quick. Lady Eliya, accompanied by others. When had he become attuned to her pace? Danek glanced over his shoulder at her, then shook his head. It would be best if she didn't inspect the bodies. And yet, she'd be the wife of Laros Rakiar of the northern realms. Rulers must never feel safe and complacent. He wouldn't lift a hand to stop her.

She approached, hugging herself, obviously physically suppressing her tremors, her golden eyes distress-widened. One step behind her, Valo stared at the slaughtered cavalcade. "Ceyphraland's colors. Someone dared attack an official cavalcade."

"Yes." Danek faced the royal siblings. Showed them the traitor-arrow. "And this is Ceyphraland yew, from the Na'Khesh Mountains. Why would anyone from Ceyphraland attack their own people?"

Valo's dark eyebrows lifted. "Is Ceyphraland mired in another civil war?"

Her troubled gaze flickering from the bodies, then up to her brother's face, Eliya murmured, "We've heard nothing of another civil war in Ceyphraland. In fact, we've heard nothing from their king in almost two months."

Danek lowered the stained arrow, hiding it from view. "Perhaps mercenaries purchased Ceyphraland weaponry for this attack."

Khelqua's princess studied the bodies again, tears glittering in her golden eyes. "These poor men. They had no time to defend themselves."

"Or no suspicion that defense was needed."

Valo stepped toward the lifeless cavalcade. "Perhaps they trusted their attackers. We shouldn't be as susceptible. I'm commanding all my men to hold their weapons near—readied even while they sleep." He looped one arm around his sister's shoulders. "Eliya, don't look at them so closely. You'll give yourself nightmares."

"I already suffer nightmares." She looked up at Danek, the evening sunlight gilding her olive-brown skin, illuminating her pale eyes. "We should gather evidence of their identities, then bury the bodies."

Gripping the polished, bloodied arrow within the folds of his cloak, Danek nodded. "I agree."

He didn't like her hushed composure. Emotional numbness often promised hysterics later. Did he misjudge her? Perhaps her preternatural calm meant that she was planning a defense.

If so, then he'd include himself in those plans. Until then, however, he'd oversee this encampment's safety. He called to his men, "Double tonight's patrols! Send two men down to Sevold Valley to order armed volunteers to join us—immediately. And before we leave, these bodies must be buried. Bring any unusual weapons or objects to me—anything to indicate this cavalcade's destination and purpose!"

If the raiders and murderers remained nearby, he must vanquish them. These killings were too close to Walhaisii lands to be ignored.

❋

ELIYA HEADED FOR HER cart and removed her exquisite crossbow case from among her most prized possessions. If she weren't so upset, she would have smiled—she could almost feel Valo's consternation as she opened the case and loaded her crossbow's bolts into their polished, high-built chamber. The evening light glinted off the elegant violet-wood recurved bow, its layers as strong as they were decorative. Like her brothers and Jesca, she'd trained as an arbalest. All healthy and able royals of Khelqua were expected to master the crossbow, complying with Khelqua's ancient traditions.

Crossbows, according to lore, had once saved the royal family from annihilation, and she and Valo were near-equals during royal competitions. He finished instructing their guards for the evening, then retrieved his own ironwood crossbow while she set up a target.

She'd just finished loading bolts into the polished chamber when the Walhaisii king approached, greeting her with an equal's nod. "Lady Eliya. I'm pleased you're obviously proficient with a crossbow. It's best to be prepared."

"Thank you for not trying to spare my fears of an attack."

"You anticipate one."

"Yes. All royals have enemies, don't they?" She lifted the crossbow and rested its carved violet-wood butt near her shoulder, then hesitated. Torena and Vaiya lingered, but not close enough to hear. "Speaking of enemies ... do you believe Aretes is following us? Or that he will return?"

The Walhaisii king's handsome face remained unreadable. "My men and I haven't seen or heard traces indicating that we're being followed. Nevertheless, it's best that we're prepared."

He seemed so calm. Was he hiding distress over the attack on Ceyphraland's people, as she was? Eliya concentrated on her target, lifted the golden lever above her crossbow's stock until the bolt clicked into place, then swiftly lowered the lever and shot a bolt. The small missile lodged gleaming and peg-like in the target's outer rim, shaming her. "I'm out of practice. But at least weapons will help us against mortal enemies. Unlike quakes and floods."

Lord-king Danek agreed, his voice low and somber as a mourners'. "Despite the Eternal Liege's prophecies, no one in this encampment believed the devastation could be so widespread."

He'd mentioned the prophecies, and the Liege. Eliya looked up at the Walhaisii lord-king. "You follow the Eternal Liege."

"Yes."

Why did the knowledge comfort her? She lifted the shining lever, setting another bolt. "Before the quake, and the flood, I would have said I wasn't wholly convinced of the Liege's claims. But seeing His prophecy so overwhelmingly fulfilled ..."

She couldn't finish. But words weren't needed. Lord-king Danek nodded, obviously understanding her inability to discuss the prophecy foretelling Khelqua's doom.

Eliya exhaled a calming breath and focused on her practice target. She mustn't think of the prophecy's pledge that Ariym would be swept away, and the king and lords would wail, helpless before the destruction. If her father and Iscah were gone, then so was Jesca. She'd ...

No. She wouldn't think of Jesca and their family. She loaded and released bolt after bolt until each shot struck near-center on the distant target.

Lord-king Danek watched her practice in silence, while Valo and Torena waited nearby. Then, he watched Valo practice as Eliya gathered her gear and returned her crossbow to its case.

Was the cryptic Walhaisii ruler determining their fitness for hunting and confronting enemies? Most likely. She couldn't blame him. Each arrow, sword, and bolt might mean the difference between victory or defeat.

She looked over at the ill-fated cavalcade, its doomed travelers now being buried by her servants and Lord Danek's men. Torena approached, her veils fluttering in the light evening wind. For one

R. J. LARSON

childish instant, Eliya longed to crawl into Torena's arms. Instead, she murmured, "Revered lady ... I wonder who killed them. And why."

"As we all do, lady." Torena's saddened glance skimmed over the lost cavalcade, then studied the landscape around them. "This has always been considered an accursed place. Somewhere within these rocks lie the ruins of ancient Parneh."

Eliya's skin chilled at the name. Parneh. A rebellious city-state doomed by a girl-prophet. Both Parneh and the girl prophet thoroughly scorned by Cyphar's chaplet-faith fanatics as mere legends. Tales told to children learning to read.

Were the legends true? These borderlands haunted one's soul—forsaken enough to persuade Eliya of their disastrous history as recorded within the Eternal's Sacred Words. "I hope we spend only one night here."

"I'm sure we will, lady," Torena answered dryly. "I, for one, won't sleep tonight. These lands were condemned long ago. Some say that the Chaplet faith originated here. Others say that it emerged far away from Khelqua, in Pheniarpas, Cyphar's birthplace."

To distract herself and shake off her creeping fears of the lands around her, Eliya asked, "Which do you believe is the truth?"

"Pheniarpas." Torena's well-bred face hardened as her voice chilled. "The Chaplet religion fit Cyphar well. For the Chaplet faithful, the Eternal is never consulted directly. Any rebellion or lust can be overlooked and 'forgiven' if one pays enough. Entire kingdoms can be murdered for a price. Even the Eternal Liege was condemned. For a price."

"I wonder ... what price was demanded to atone for murdering this royal cavalcade?"

Shivering, Eliya returned her crossbow's case to her storage cart, but kept her crossbow close. She clambered inside her luxuriously gilded violet wagon and washed her hands and face. Finished, she sat on one of the narrow, deeply cushioned beds and allowed Torena and Vaiya to unpin and comb her hair while she stared at the flower-and-vine-painted ceiling. True, they were traveling, but she mustn't look like some refugee. Even if she felt like one. What was Jesca doing? And Father?

As Vaiya began to plait her hair, Eliya said, "If only we'd news of Ariym and the northern lands."

"Indeed, lady." Vaiya smoothed one long strand of Eliya's hair, then continued plaiting. Her voice wavering, Vaiya confessed, "I keep telling myself that the entire river valley *can't* be flooded."

Yet Ariym was nearer to sea level than the now-drowned plains. No. Eliya closed her eyes and resisted the thought. Ariym must have survived the flood. Seated adjacent to Eliya in her own cushioned, quilt-draped bed, Torena's dark eyes reflected sorrow—unspoken certainty that their hopes were wasted.

Outside her wagon's partially opened door, a hunter's horn sounded in the distance. But shouts from guardsmen and the clatter of weapons belied a mere hunter's call. Eliya tugged her hair from Vaiya's grasp and stood. "Something's happened. We'll finish my hair later."

"May I tie it for now, lady? Just one knot."

"Thank you." Eliya waited, listening to the commotion outside. Men's warning-sharp whistles and another horn's blare sounded. Torena edged toward the back of the wagon, stepped through the doorway, then descended the wooden ladder. The instant Vaiya released her, Eliya seized her crossbow and descended from the wagon. As she met up with Torena, Valo stalked past them, holding his crossbow readied. Eliya rushed to catch up with him. "What's happened?"

Valo grimaced and flicked his golden gaze from her to the clearing ahead. "I heard the warning call, then saw one of the Walhaisii run to bow before Lord-king Danek. I'm sure his men found something."

They approached the impressively grim Danek, who approved their weapons with a sidelong look and a nod. Three Walhaisii guardsmen hurried into the clearing, half-dragging a rough-clad bowman among them. The lead guardsman bowed his head, then motioned toward their captive. "Here's an unusual object for you, my lord. We caught sight of him spying out the valley beyond the ruins and chased him down."

The two subordinate guardsmen shoved their prisoner onto his knees before Danek, and the lead guard swept a plain wooden arrow from the rustic quiver that rested over the prisoner's back. Eliya glanced at the arrow's shimmering red-gold grain. This marauder had evidently participated in slaughtering the ill-fated cavalcade. The prisoner's bewhiskered, sun-bronzed face tensed. He looked from Danek to her, then froze. His brown eyes widening, the captive stared at Eliya as if seeing some incredible thing he'd heard of, but never expected to see.

How did this foreigner recognize her? From another's description, undoubtedly. But had he been searching for her?

Before Danek could say a word, Eliya accused the man. "Somehow, you've heard of me. You've expected my cavalcade."

The prisoner looked away. But not before she saw a shadow of acknowledgement flick over his rough-shaven face. Valo asked, "Is this true?"

When the man remained stubbornly silent, Danek reached down, grasped the man's wrist, then wrenched his entire arm backward and up, twisting it at the shoulder, making the prisoner gasp. "You will lose this arm if you don't comply. Tell us!"

The Walhaisii lord-king lifted the captive's arm higher and more sharply until the man yelled. "Stop-stop ... !"

Danek growled, the noise low and savage in his throat. "Talk, or you lose your arm!"

The prisoner bellowed, "You'll die if you don't release me! They're planning another attack!"

"On our cavalcade?"

Through bared, gritted teeth, the man snarled, "Yes!"

Danek adjusted the man's arm, provoking another pained yell. Eliya fought the instinct to look away. To plead for mercy. The man was a killer—he'd all but admitted it. As the prisoner hushed again, the Walhaisii lord-king spoke, low and savage, as if he'd tear into the man's flesh like an animal. "Who is this lady to you?"

"Dead! Unless you release me!"

Danek leaned down and bellowed into the man's ear, "*Where* are your comrades?"

The captive squirmed beneath Danek's grasp. "Searching for me, soon enough!"

"Whom do you serve?"

"I'll swallow my own tongue before saying more!"

Straightening slightly, Danek wrenched the man's arm, provoking one last yell. Danek flung the prisoner to the ground, then ordered his lead guard. "Take his weapons. Strip him down to his slops, then chase him from camp."

As his guards obeyed, stripping the thrashing, raging captive, Danek firmly steered Eliya and Valo away. Beyond the prisoner's earshot, Danek muttered, "My men will follow him. I'm convinced he's heard a description of Khelqua's princess, and his comrades plan to capture her. Within a day, we'll know."

Capture? Eliya huffed out a frustrated breath. "Who'd dare to risk Tetrarch Rakiar's anger by capturing me? They'd have half the empire hunting them."

Lord-king Danek grumbled, his rich voice comforting despite the uncomfortable topic of her safety. "Anyone crack-skulled enough to snatch you won't survive the attempt. If all goes well, my reinforcements should arrive tomorrow morning. Tonight, we keep watch and pray."

Torena approved the Walhaisii lord-king's verdict with a silent nod, then a quizzing glance at Eliya.

Did her revered mentor suspect her growing admiration for the Walhaisii lord-king?

Eliya looked away.

Nearby, in the looming dusk, their men finished burying Ceyphraland's dead. While placing the last rocks over the makeshift cairn, the Walhaisii began to croon out a tune, low and lulling. The tune deepened, gaining force and wordless emotion, the raw notes chilling Eliya's flesh as she listened. She couldn't look away from the Walhaisii, Danek now among them, all lifting their hands and faces to the darkening skies, closing their eyes, their voices soaring upward toward the Eternal, wailing their formless anguish and innocence over Ceyphraland's murdered citizens.

Tears burned Eliya's gaze, blurring the night's first stars.

Unasked, Torena and Vaiya encircled her in their arms, crying with her as they mourned this journey's losses.

※

DANEK WATCHED THE PREDAWN shadows shift, then brighten in the far edge of the clearing. At least forty burly and suspicious Sevold Valley men rode surefooted golden horses into the desolate open fields, each man exemplifying the warrior-silence and stamina of their highland ancestors.

Danek's lord-father and all their kindred claimed deep ties and loyalties to the clans of the sprawling Sevold Valley—its citizens among the few Walhaisii untroubled by their nearness to accursed Parneh's supposedly haunted ancient lands.

Sevold fighters were the most difficult Walhaisii to trouble. Or to conquer.

Danek muted a sigh of relief as they approached.

The Lady Eliya would be safe. And he'd sleep for an hour or two while the Sevold warriors watered their horses from Parneh's ancient wells, then ate their morning meal. Their leader, Sion—a giant of a man who insisted he was Danek's distant cousin—dropped from his horse and grinned. "My lord, how did you know we were bored?"

Danek returned his grin. "You Sevolds are always bored."

"We heard rumors you were heading toward Parneh. Why?"

"I promised Rodiades of Khelqua that I'd take his eldest daughter and his second son safely through Walhaisii lands."

Obviously baffled, Sion pushed his big hand through his dark, untamed hair. "So? Parneh's wilds are beyond Walhaisii lands. Your pledge is satisfied."

"Not if I leave my charges among marauders." He nodded toward the doomed cavalcade, abandoned and desolate, just beyond the princess' still drowsing encampment of wagons and tents. "We spent yesterday evening burying corpses. I need to ensure that Khelqua's young royals aren't murdered as well."

Sion grimaced, then nodded. "That might give me pause if I were walking your path, my lord. We'll deliver them safe to ... where?"

"Laros Rakiar of Trisguard."

"I thought you said we wouldn't leave them among marauders."

Undoubtedly Sion spoke in jest, but his taunt sharpened Danek's fears. "I've heard Rakiar called many things, but he's not known as a marauder."

Yet.

*

DISMOUNTING A SAFE distance from the edge of the cliff, Aretes, former commander of the third royal regiment of Ariym, beheld the newborn death-dark sea and gauged its waves and breadth compared to the far foothills. Those sea-lapped slopes framed Ariym's river valley, guarding the mountain passes. The mountains loomed in the distance, bleak and dark gray, promising difficult passage to the far-away sacred city of Pheniarpas.

The flood waters lapped the far foothills. Ariym was drowned.

Khelqua was dead.

Aretes screamed until his agony echoed against the nearby hillsides, then shut his eyes against the onslaught of tears. He must give up hope. Reckoning and desolation had swept over his homeland, just as those verse-spouting cultist fanatics had proclaimed ... echoing that legally reprobate Liege they revered as the Eternal.

The prophecy lay before him, proven.

Two choices emerged from Aretes' dazed grief. He could follow the Liege, and the Rone'en's fanatics, or—

He turned his back on Khelqua's flooded grave.

A coincidence. He must believe the flood a coincidence or go insane.

Thus, his allegiances changed through no subterfuge of his own. What choice did he have? Would his new lord reward him for this news or kill him for it?

He'd learn soon enough.

What was the swiftest, surest route through the Walhaisii mountains?

Goading his horse away from the fatal sea and its appalling coincidental destruction, Aretes rode downslope through the trees. At a turn on a rain-washed hillside, he risked one more glance toward Khelqua's grave. How could Ariym be gone? Its splendors vanquished? His gaze slid from the distant ocean to surprisingly clean-swept paths below. To a storm-shredded banner dangling from a tree over the remains of a makeshift camp. Tumbled logs, debris, and the corpses of a horse and a Khelqua guardsman lay snarled amid the leavings of a fatal inland tide.

Lord Valo's search party. They'd camped too low in the valley and were overtaken by an unexpected flood. Good men lost, searching for hope from their devastated realm.

Willing back a madman's wild screams, Aretes turned his horse toward higher paths, heading east—as swiftly as his and his horse's strength allowed.

❋

ELIYA GATHERED HER mantle in one hand, her crossbow in the other, and then stepped down from her wagon into the darkness.

Sleep, when it overtook her, offered horrors. Bodies floating among Ariym's ruins, herself among them, fighting to hold her last breath while murky water stole her unformed tears.

Breathing in tonight's chilly air, she walked past the watchmen toward the shadowed blade-like stone formations sheltering tonight's encampment. Tall stones curved around her promising solitude and sanctuary—a natural temple in the darkness. There, walled away from the world among the spires, she halted and stared up at the stars. At the Eternal's endless robe of glittering night.

To Him, she whispered, "You're here. I sense You. Why do You seem so close tonight? If only I could receive Your thoughts, as a prophet of old. If I could have warned everyone …."

No one in Khelqua would have listened. When were prophets ever trusted or allowed to live to old age? Better to be an ordinary mortal. Yet, if only—

A thin current of air skimmed past her cheek, touching her face, alerting her senses, halting her where she stood. Something intangible lingered beyond the warning, protective, near-whispering current.

All the hairs prickled across Eliya's forearms. By instinct, she lifted her crossbow toward the shadows. Forms took shape, unfurling in the darkness as wings swept back to reveal faces. Taunting, mocking, leering faces, their dark eyes deflecting light.

Eliya shot a bolt into the shadows. The unfurled creatures loomed untouched, mocking her, their lightless gazes multiplying—a fathomless army's loathsome night watch. Her heartbeat racing, she begged, "Eternal Liege, banish them!"

The current gusted toward those otherworldly watchers, and the shadows fled, skimming away over the rocks, seeping into the darkness.

Eliya knelt, countless unformed prayers muddled within her thoughts. Who would believe her, if she told anyone of this?

She waited until her breath and heartbeat slowed, then staggered to her feet and left the spires' solitude.

Khelqua's guards turned toward her as she approached, bored, yet alert to everything mortals usually saw. Obviously, they'd heard nothing amiss.

Torena sat on the wagon's lowest step, waiting for her. "Lady, are you ill?"

"Yes. And I doubt I'll recover for years."

Avoiding her teacher's too-sharp gaze, she entered the wagon and hid herself in a pretense of sleep.

✳

RIDING BESIDE TORENA amid the deepening shadows cast by rock spires and crags above, Eliya loosened her veiled, broad-brimmed hat and let it dangle down her back. No need to ward off a sunburn here. Though tonight's scenery offered plenty of fearsome images amid this endless, nightmarishly long journey. "I've come to dread the evenings. Terrible things always occur just as we build our camp for the night. Where do you suppose we are?"

Her veiled silver hair gleaming in the fading light, Torena looked around and quoted, "'The Eternal sent His prophet into a wilderness, to understand His Spirit and comprehend His ways. To trust Him, even to death. May His servants bless Him forever.' These must be the renowned lands of testing. In other words, I believe we'll soon reach the border. Trisguard lies beyond these lands of forsaken stones and briars."

These were the lands of testing? Eliya studied the reddened rocks, now shadowed with violets and gray-blues. What traits were tested in these renowned lands during ancient times? A willingness to seek the Eternal? Perhaps ... to listen. Or to trust. Was she being tested? She sensed His tranquility, surrounded by such desolation. He beckoned. If only she could forget everything facing her, and everything she'd lost in Khelqua and Ariym.

She closed her eyes, allowing her horse to merely follow the cavalcade's chosen route. Articulating her prayer in only the faintest threads of sound, lest her words echo off the rocks, she whispered to the Eternal, "Are You testing me? Weighing my heart? Yet if I accept You ... trust You ... haven't You pledged to be my refuge?"

Torena's voice seeped into her prayer. "What, Lady? Did you say something?"

Eliya opened her eyes. "I was praying."

"Forgive me." Torena bowed her head, then looked away.

Was she embarrassed? Eliya smiled, then shrugged. "My prayer was finished—no reason to ask forgiveness. But, Torena ...?"

"Yes?"

"What will we do if the persecution has spread to Trisguard? If Trisguard's Chaplet faithful are supported by Rakiar, then we'd be in danger despite my rank."

Torena edged her meek palfrey closer, lowering her voice. "Is that a confession of faith, lady?"

Tears blurred Eliya's gaze—unexpected, weakening, yet somehow right. Her words shook, though barely above a whisper. "I sense the Eternal so strongly here. Don't you?"

"Always. Though, I admit I'm not the best of witnesses for Him."

Not the best of witnesses? Her dignified teacher? Eliya allowed herself a bleak laugh. "You are!"

Torena almost snorted. "Hardly. You might have guessed by my debates with Kiyros that I enjoy conflict. Indeed, I'm not as gentle and forgiving as the Sacred Word commands me to be."

"That's not how you seem to others." Eliya took up the argument, attempting to forget her recent spiritual misadventure, and her longing to escape into this wilderness. Not even Torena would approve of such folly. "You've always been a spiritual puzzlement to me, my revered teacher. I know that you trust the Eternal Liege, and the Rone'en above the Chaplet faith. And I'm convinced that for all your debates, Kiyros is of the Chaplet faith. What puzzles me is that most teachers wouldn't routinely bring the opposition into a classroom and allow them to say whatever they please. Why did you?"

Torena shrugged. "I trust my Divine Teacher, and your own powers of discernment, lady. Not to mention your strength of character. I've always felt that if I didn't present both sides of an argument, I'd lose your esteem."

"True again." Eliya studied the dusty rock-strewn path ahead. "And I suppose that Kiyros reassured the entire court that I'm dedicated to the ruling Chaplet faith of Khelqua." Had someone offered Laros Rakiar a similar reassurance?

Distant hunting horns blared sonorous alarms off the rock spires ahead, the echoes roiling up and down the rock-hedged road like a physical wave. Eliya reached down and lifted her sleek crossbow from its strap on her saddle. She'd loaded ten bolts into the high-built chamber, but none of the bolts were poisoned as recommended for battle. Would this confrontation become a battle?

Lord-king Danek's formidable Sevold fighters formed ranks on either side of Eliya's household, their lines reaching Valo and his men as well, though one glance at Valo informed Eliya of her brother's irritation at the Walhaisii lord-king's presumption that he couldn't fend for himself.

She'd talk with Valo later. Danek had pledged his protection, and one mustn't scorn a man honoring his own word. As long as the pledge wasn't ....

Eliya's plans faded, banished by invaders.

Foreign mounted regiments, weathered, toughened men clad in Ceyphraland red and gold, rode into the open area on the path ahead. Behind them, cavalrymen flaunting Belvasae's brilliant blue and gold colors urged their horses into formation with Ceyphraland's vivid ranks.

Swallowing against nausea, Eliya lowered her crossbow. These cold-eyed soldiers weren't ruffians she and her household could simply shoot upon and chase away. What sort of attack was this? Did these men realize this was her wedding cavalcade? If so, why would half the empire officially halt her procession? Worse ... She, Valo, and Danek must tell these Ceyphraland soldiers that some of their own citizens had been ambushed in a cavalcade.

Would the Ceyphralanders accuse them of the attack?

Vaiya rode up beside Eliya, her delicate tawny-pink face tensed beneath its shading veils. "Lady, what should I do?"

Aware of Valo and Lord-king Danek riding forward, Eliya gathered her horse's reins. "Wait. And pray."

She urged her horse out of formation. To confront the allied blockade.

Chapter 4

Danek tightened his grip on his horse's reins to prevent himself from chasing Lady Eliya back into the comparative safety of their own men.

How could he allow her to ride into that waiting formation of imperial predators?

If only he could snatch her into the shadows, and hide her in his realm, the humblest and least civilized people of all in the empire. At least she'd be safe for a time. She'd faced enough distress on this journey, and considering the glares of those grim-faced soldiers ahead, she was about to face more. Perhaps they'd all endure threats when these imperial soldiers learned of the recent attack on the Ceyphralanders' cavalcade.

Aware of his own men subtly shifting their hands to their varied bows and swords, Danek guided his horse alongside Valo's wearied gray, then spoke as low as possible. "Lord-prince, we're beyond my lands, so it's up to you to encourage peaceable rapport among our fellow-citizens of the empire."

Valo gusted out an impatient breath. "Obviously! But what can they possibly want?"

"Perhaps they're seeking the Ceyphraland cavalcade."

The young prince tensed, aging before Danek's gaze. Tight-voiced, Valo told Danek, "Guard my sister if I'm killed."

"I'd prefer to think we'll survive." Yet, if he, Danek, should die, what would happen to the Walhaisii?

He mustn't waste his energies on imagining disasters that could only happen after his death. Hadn't the Liege preached in the Walhaisii foothills against borrowing trouble? He couldn't change one hair on his own head by fretting over what couldn't be helped—or by imagining calamities that might never happen.

Danek willed himself to relax and concentrate on the wall of soldiers arrayed before them. Obviously, Ceyphraland and Belvasae had deliberately chosen this show of joint force, though a ceremonial envoy with a decorative retinue wouldn't have been as alarming to a royal cavalcade.

Before Valo could utter a word, Eliya called to the allied forces of east and south in exactly the right mix of regal indignation and bewilderment, "Sirs, I am Eliyana of Ariym, daughter of Rodiades the tetrarch of Khelqua. What's happened? Why are Khelqua's allies interfering with my wedding journey?"

As soon as she pronounced her name and her father's name, the allied commanders and their men bowed their heads in brief, formal acknowledgement of her status. And, thank the Eternal, obvious respect for her rank. Even so, the most gold-decked of Ceyphraland's crimson uniformed commanders lifted a gloved hand to halt her. "Lady, we were commanded to invite you to a council—an inquiry of Ceyfraland and Belvasae—before you cross the border into Trisguard. The council waits for you in the plains beyond us."

Valo leaned forward, his voice surprisingly cold and authoritative. "Do you command my royal sister, sirs, or is she invited of her own free will?" Before they could ask, Valo added, "I am Lord-prince Valo of Ariym, second son of Tetrarch Rodiades of Khelqua, and my sister and I have the honor of being accompanied by Lord-king Danek of the Walhaisii. And his men."

Valo bowed his head, acknowledging Danek's higher status. Slight shifts threaded among the commanders and their subordinates like the uneasy stirrings of a cobweb caught in a breeze.

Compelling the lead commander to hold his gaze, and allowing his own irritation to show, Danek took advantage of their adversaries' fresh uncertainties. "Whatever happens, sirs, we must inform you of unwelcomed news. Recently, we found an ambushed cavalcade from Ceyphraland—its citizens had been dead for several days, so we buried them and collected documentation and evidence for your lord-king. The cavalcade's remains await your inspection in the plains just west of ancient Parneh. We offer our condolences for your country's losses, and invite any further questions."

The two commanders traded looks and sharply whispered words. At last, Belvasae's commander shrugged. Ceyphraland's commander motioned five men forward. "Go. Find the cavalcade and bring a full report to the king."

His expression flat, remote, the Ceyphraland commander dismounted and bowed his head. "Lord-king of the Walhaisii, we thank you for the warning. As pertaining to my primary mission: please ride with us. I give you my oath that this council will benefit you and Khelqua. My lord, Aniketos, tetrarch of the eastern realm of Ceyphraland and his heir, Adalric of Rhyve, will certainly request the favor of your presence. As will Belkrates, tetrarch of the southern realm of Belvasae, and his heir, Belkian."

Danek's very being stilled. What brought the empire's allied rulers together in the most desolate plot on the continent? He could not refuse their forced invitation. Nor could Eliya or Valo.

Eliya reined back her horse as if unsettled, but she addressed the lead commander coolly. "What about my betrothed, Laros Rakiar, tetrarch of the northern realm of Trisguard?"

"Messengers have been sent to inform him of the council. Lady, night approaches. Please, accept the empire's invitation. We've no wish to battle you or ..." He bowed to Danek. "...the Walhaisii."

A delicate grimace played over Eliya's face, but she half-nodded, then swept a glance toward Danek and Valo, obviously seeking their opinions.

Danek exhaled, then shrugged. Was the Lady Eliya's pending marriage of such great concern to Belvasae and Ceyphraland? Or were the imperial lord-kings maneuvering them all like pieces in some deceitful game of their own?

＊

SHIFTING WITHIN HER saddle to ease her fatigue, Eliya studied the sprawling torch and lamp-lit encampment ahead. Its air of slumberous quiet reassured her. Yet weapon-wielding guards rimmed the camp as she and her exhausted cavalcade rode in, led by Ceyphraland's torch-bearing foot-soldiers. In the camp's center, more guards encircled two truly regal crimson and blue tents that glowed from within. Regiments of men could fit within those tents—not to mention the empire's rulers and chief courtiers.

What grand schemes had the eastern and southern tetrarchs concocted?

As Eliya descended from her palfrey, Valo hurried to meet her and to whisper, "Now we'll learn if we're guests or prisoners."

"Oh, I'd guess we're prisoners. Why should we expect anything wonderful after all that's happened on my wedding journey!"

"You're right." Valo's voice was half-mirth, half-gloom in the darkness. "This is all your fault." He gave her a bracing hug, then shook her lightly. "But, I forgive you—no matter what disaster you've led me into."

Danek stalked over to join them as his horse was led away by his men. Even in the dark, Eliya saw his brooding mistrust of their hosts. "Have the lowland lord-kings quarreled with your betrothed?"

Watching their imperial guards forming ranks once more at the camp's edge, Eliya whispered, "If they've quarreled, I haven't heard of it. As far as we knew, they were all on good terms when I left Ariym. My lord-father communicated with the other tetrarchs routinely."

"Until recently," Valo reminded her. "Before we left, Father complained that we'd heard very little from the other realms since before Rakiar offered for you in marriage."

True. Had there been a falling out among the other tetrarchs? Eliya scowled. "Look—our guards are about to take charge of us again. Any advice, Walhaisii?"

Danek grumbled, "Be wary of the empire's politics—say as little as possible. And prepare for snow. There's a breath of winter in the air."

Pessimism and predictions of a storm from the Walhaisii highlands ruler. Well. The weather *was* approaching from his own realm. Eliya called to Torena and Vaiya, "Please bring our winter cloaks, then remain near."

Ceyphraland's guards halted, and their red-garbed commander bowed. "Your presence is expected in Ceyphraland's tent."

"As soon as I've received my cloak," Eliya promised. While the men shuffled and traded impatient looks, she fixed her gaze upward, on the stars, watching them vanish behind a misted haze-like fog. Her winter cloak and Valo's, unlike their owners, would be clean, beautiful, and worthy of being presented before the joint rulers of the Syvlande Empire. Her lord-father would agree they must be neat despite their journey. Even if this coerced meeting might send him into a royal rage.

Sooner than she'd expected, Torena and Vaiya returned, wearing their own winter cloaks and carrying hers and Valo's. Obviously impatient, Valo snatched his cloak and swung it over his shoulders, careless of its gilded clasps. Eliya hid a smile. If only donning apparel could be so simple. She must wait and allow her ladies their work.

While Vaiya shook out its gold-embroidered, sable-edged purple-wool folds, Torena whisked away Eliya's travel hat and veil, then replaced it with a simple gold circlet. She hurriedly combed back Eliya's hair, then helped Vaiya fasten the heavy cloak over Eliya's shoulders. Eliya whispered to them, "I wish I could carry weapons."

"You'll be surrounded by our prayers to the Eternal," Torena promised.

"Thank you. Pray for the others in attendance as well."

Her teacher's eyes widened in the misty darkness. "Lady, remember: let your thoughts be disciplined, your words few and well-chosen."

In other words, don't lose her temper. "I'll pretend I'm facing Kiyros during lessons. Did I ever lose patience with him?"

"No, but you routinely provoked him, and these men aren't mere teachers!"

Valo reached for Eliya's hand. "Torena's right, and we've delayed too long. Enough stalling—one would think you're afraid."

One would be right. However ... "I wasn't stalling." She lifted their linked hands as if they were two fighters pledged to the same team. "May blessings emerge from this meeting."

"Yes, if that makes you feel better." Valo started toward the huge tent. Eliya tugged him to a halt. Valo glared. "What now? You *are* afraid."

"Fear's not why I stopped you." Eliya stepped aside and glanced at Danek. "We should proceed in order of rank."

"As you say." The Walhaisii lord-king strode ahead, evidently determined to charge into the meeting and finish it as quickly as possible.

The guard announced their names—his full and authoritative voice drowning any polite conversation inside the huge tent. "Lord-king Danek of the Walhaisii. Lord-prince Valo of Ariym and Khelqua, and his sister, the Lady Eliyana of Ariym and Khelqua!"

Everyone stared, obviously curious—a highborn crowd bored with its own company. Could they actually be nothing more than a pack of spoiled royal idlers who'd journeyed to this wilderness for mere amusement? Eliya smiled, allowing her dark amusement to show. Yet, she must behave. At least Valo looked dignified. And regally handsome—worthy to stand among the royals facing them now.

Lord-king Aniketos, tetrarch of the eastern realm of Ceyphraland, stood and stared at her—his rank and country emphasized by the gold circlet on his yellow-white hair, and the Ceyphraland red and gold of his sweeping tunic and cloak. His reddened, rheumy eyelids sagged over his gray eyes, his broken-veined face implying a man wearied of life. Nothing like the determined, vigorous signature he'd routinely inked onto imperial documents sent to Khelqua.

Aniketos studied Eliya and Valo, then his glance shifted to Danek and turned remote. As if he'd donned a mask of courtesy. Clearing his throat, Aniketos nodded toward Danek, Valo, and Eliya. "On behalf of Ceyphraland, and my heir, Adalric of Rhyve, we welcome you."

He flicked a careless hand toward a taller, younger, healthier version of himself. Adalric of Rhyve briefly bowed his head, then met Eliya's gaze, frankly interested.

Another gold-crowned and imposing royal stepped toward Aniketos, then nodded at Danek, his dark blue and gold robes and weathered skin informing Eliya that she'd just met Belkrates, tetrarch of the southern realm of Belvasae. "Welcome to all on behalf of Belvasae. Thank you for attending us."

Unlike Aniketos, Belkrates didn't bother to introduce his heir. But beside him, a bored, dark-haired adolescent, with much the same thin physique, shifted from foot to foot as if he'd rather not attend this gathering. Were the rumors of Belkian, lord-prince of Belvasae true? Had the young lord truly fallen in love with a commoner? If so, was he fighting with his father to have her brought into the royal family?

Adalric of Rhyve cleared his throat, bringing Eliya's attention toward him. Again, he gave her an appraising glance. Presumptuous. Ignoring him, she bowed toward both tetrarchs, then straightened. "My lords. We're interested in your reasons for halting my wedding cavalcade. And ... we bring you news."

Aniketos lifted one hand. "Let's be seated and allow our food to be served. Then we'll discuss your news."

Servants brought unexpectedly comfortable red cushions, sang brief Chaplet worship prayers, then presented silver trays of food. Soft, pale bread, roasted lamb, fiery red sauces, dried fruits, and numerous choices of fried, boiled, and baked eggs. A springtime feast she'd no appetite for. Eliya forced herself to eat.

Belkrates picked at his food, and just as fussily, quizzed Valo and Danek for the news. Obviously, princess or not, Eliya was a female, unlikely to know anything important.

In sparse yet sympathetic terms, Danek described the devastated Ceyphraland cavalcade, adding, "I am sorry. My men are guarding the documents and valuables we found as we buried the dead—we'll have them brought to you, Lord-king Aniketos, as soon as this meeting ends. No sealed boxes or parchments were opened, and we honored the dead with prayers and hymns. We'll gladly answer any further questions."

Around the tent, courtiers' whispers and aggrieved expressions matched Aniketos' bleakness. The eastern tetrarch set down his gilded goblet and exhaled. "Thus, I've lost an ambassador and some of my country's finest clerks and servants."

He lapsed into brooding silence, but slowly continued to eat. Belkrates toyed with a morsel of bread while Valo, seated beside Eliya, described Khelqua's flood. Tremors shook Eliya, as the remembered death scents of humid air and broken soil evoked her country's loss. She set aside her half-eaten food. As did Aniketos.

At last, after working his tongue over his teeth, either freeing half-chewed crumbs or biting back words, Ceyphraland's lord-king sighed, then shook his head. "It seems my ambassador and servants would have been dispatched to the Eternal even if they'd reached their destination. Yet, natural or divinely predicted disasters must be accepted. Murderous mortals, however, are quite another matter."

He gazed at Eliya for such a long moment that she almost forgot her grief over remembering the flood. "Eliyana of Ariym and Khelqua, we sent our servants—for the third time—to request that you marry my son. My first two messengers were never heard from again. And you saw the fate of the most recent ones."

He'd sent three messengers? "That was the cavalcade's mission?" Eliya swallowed. She'd been the indirect cause of all those deaths. Blinking down the first hints of tears, she managed, "We received no correspondence from Ceyphraland concerning marriage. Only from Trisguard."

"Obviously." Belkrates carelessly set a golden goblet onto his silver tray, allowing it to clatter. Then he spoke to the air above Eliya's head. "This past year, two of my own messengers were lost to the wilderness around ancient Parneh. Those lands were ever a curse to us." He lifted his chin at Valo. "What of Ariym? When do you expect to hear news of your lord-father?"

Valo handed an emptied dish to a servant. "If our messengers travel swiftly with no delays, we should greet them within a few days. Though I told them to meet us at the designated gathering place beyond Trisguard's border."

Aniketos said, "They will be met. As will Laros Rakiar." He looked at Eliya. "Trisguard did not request our permission for your marriage, lady."

Could these two infuriated tetrarchs dissolve her marriage contract? Did she want them to dissolve the contract? She wouldn't be intimidated. Chin up, Eliya kept her voice low and neutral. "I didn't realize. Again, his was the only realm that requested me."

"That your lord-father knew of." Aniketos coughed.

"Yes. We hope your lost messengers return soon." An unlikely hope.

Had Laros Rakiar ordered his rivals' messengers intercepted and killed?

She dared not ask aloud. Yet there was no need—she saw her unspoken question reflected in both tetrarchs' eyes.

Amid a furtive hum of low-voiced comments from courtiers around the tent, Valo leaned toward her and whispered, "Better we endure this meeting now, than war against half the empire later."

"True. I don't believe we're being blamed for the messengers disappearing." Eliya studied the onlookers from beneath her lashes, trying to discern their mood. As she watched, a hitherto unobtrusive young noblewoman stood amid Ceyphraland's still-whispering courtiers, splendid in gold-embroidered crimson, her dark flowing curls veiled, her extraordinary silver-eyed gaze fixed on Eliya and Valo.

Her rich crimson robes gently sweeping past others as she walked, the young noblewoman approached Eliya and Valo, then knelt between them. "Please excuse my possible rudeness. But if I wait for my uncle to remember to introduce me, I'll be silver-haired or dead before we meet. I am Valeria Lantes, niece of my dear Lord-king Aniketos."

This pleasant young lady was Aniketos' niece? Moreover, judging by the fond look the girl cast toward Aniketos, she genuinely loved and admired her uncle. Eliya almost winced. Apparently, she'd judged Aniketos too harshly. Even now, Aniketos paused amid a hushed conversation with his heir and made a wry face at his niece. Trading him glance for jesting glance, Valeria wrinkled her small nose mischievously, then laughed. "See! Now he's remembered. But I don't blame my lord-uncle. He's been troubled by too many matters of state these past few months. Listen ..."

She leaned toward Eliya. "I've heard you've been sleeping in your wagon during your journey. Would you and your ladies like to share my tent while you're here? We're quite outnumbered by the men. We might as well join forces. What do you say?"

Eliya smiled. Her beautiful violet and gold wagon, with its small tile-shielded iron stove and thickly cushioned beds, might prove warmer tonight if Lord-king Danek was correct about the coming storm. But she and Torena and Vaiya needed cheerful company. Grief and bleak memories of Khelqua hovered too near each night. "Thank you—yes."

She glanced at Valo for his silent opinion.

He was gazing at Valeria as if she'd placed the world at his feet.

✹

CRUSTS OF ICE BROKE under Eliya's boots as she walked with Valeria to the central tent for morning meal. Snow, deep as her fingers were long, cloaked the ground and all undisturbed objects. Snow in Khelqua's low river valley was rare. Too rare—she'd always enjoyed it as a child, and mourned as it melted away. Danek certainly had a knack for predicting storms. She'd compliment him this morning.

Her teasing silvery gaze bright, Valeria tugged Eliya's arm. "Slow down! Now that we're not surrounded by everyone, I want to warn you ... *they* plan to break your betrothal. My lord-uncle wants you to wed my cousin Adalric. If that's true we'll be cousins."

Break her betrothal? Eliya lifted her eyebrows. "How can they break a legal and religious contract binding me to Laros Rakiar? And wouldn't Belvasae object either way?"

"Ceyphraland is mightier than Belvasae, so Belkrates won't be able to muster enough opposition. Besides, I've heard that Belkian's secretly married. And what does it matter if Laros Rakiar objects? If your lord-father signed a contract, some clever Ceyphraland cleric will find a weak clause and declare it void. Or pay an open hand among the Chaplet hierarchy that's willing to accept a bribe to break the agreement. Not that I approve."

Valo crossed their path and grinned, then waited. Valeria tilted her head toward Eliya and murmured, "What I wish my family *would* do is plan my own marriage. To someone like your handsome brother. What if—"

Several more men halted and waited with Valo. Ceyphraland's smiling lord-king, and his heir, Adalric. Catching her glance, Adalric grinned—wearing the satisfied look of a man planning to best an unseen foe.

Did he loathe Laros Rakiar?

Would she?

Standing just beyond the other men, Danek watched her. When she met his gaze, he looked away.

Until Adalric stepped forward, his brown eyes shining, admiring Eliya openly. "Well-met, cousin, and Lady Eliya. The snow, being warmed by such beauty, is bound to melt off by midday. Meanwhile, I pray to the Eternal and all the powers that be, to have Rakiar's supply wagons frozen and all his roads unpassable for a week."

"Why a week?" Eliya demanded.

"Because ..." Adalric lifted her hand without asking permission, then held it firmly within his gloved fingers. "Anything can happen within a week." Lowering his voice, he added, "If I weren't convinced I'd start a war, I'd steal you and run. Let the north deal with that."

Eliya managed a smile. But his words nagged, even as his gaze measured her reaction. Did he actually intend to steal her? As if she were property.

She must talk to Valo. Adalric's flirting wasn't the only troublesome aspect of this 'visit' among the tetrarchs. Couriers wearing military insignias from Ceyphraland and Belvasae appeared with unnerving frequency. Each courier offered their respective tetrarch parchments and whispered messages, then vanished as swiftly as they'd appeared, evidently running relays throughout half the empire. Military couriers signified more than routine talks among tetrarchs. The Syvlande Empire seemed restless as a bees' hive preparing to swarm, and she'd no warning of where the dark nettlesome cloud might descend.

❋

ELIYA SHIVERED BENEATH her heap of quilts and furs, then squirmed to find a comfortable position on her pallet. The first night she slept here, she'd been so tired that she fell asleep instantly. Now, on this second night, thick as the padding was, the ground beneath was lumpy and rocky and she felt every small pebble and every knotted tuft of trampled weeds. Tomorrow night—actually tonight, for dawn was undoubtedly a short time away—she'd invite Valeria to stay in her comfortable, richly appointed wagon.

Sooner than she expected, Eliya watched the air brighten outside the tent. Dawn neared. She would give up on sleep, sneak outside to the privy, and then prepare for the day. Except that she'd brought her clothes and grooming gear into Valeria's tent last night, and she might wake the other ladies from their well-deserved rest. Ah, well. She'd give up on facing the day early. But at least she could sneak out to a privy.

She sat up and reached for her robe. Instantly, Valeria sat up and whispered, "Oh, good! You're awake—the light woke me. How can it be morning? Actually, dawn shone yesterday from the other direction. Something's amiss."

They pulled on their outer robes and boots, scooted from Valeria's admittedly fine tent and looked toward the unexpected source of light—just as men's voices bellowed throughout the camp, "Fire! Save the ladies!"

Eliya halted in the tent's entry, staring as fire consumed her beautiful violet and gold wagon.

Chapter 5

Beneath an inappropriately tranquil blue morning sky, Eliya stood with Valeria and watched as servants picked through the tilted, charred, sodden remains of her ruined wagon. Valeria hugged herself, obviously still distressed. "Have you lost many irreplaceable things?"

Irreplaceable? Her boots, slippers, and medicinals were destroyed, but could be replaced. Her writing gear, too, was replaceable. However ... "My books. Notes from Jesca and Father ..."

Valeria's beautiful silvery eyes misted, their dark-lashed edges shimmering with unshed tears. "I'm so sorry. Notes from loved ones are more precious than gold. If I lost my parents' notes, now that I'm orphaned, it would be like another death." She gave Eliya a fierce, brief hug. "Thankfully, some of your most precious belongings are in my tent."

"Yes. What a mercy that your ladies demanded to see my bridal goods." Her gems, money and wedding-week clothes, all rested safe near her sleeping gear in Valeria's tent, along with most of Torena and Vaiya's belongings. "But how could a fire consume my wagon if the stove wasn't kindled last night?"

Valo emerged from the small throng of servants and stalked toward Eliya, his dark-whiskered face grim, one hand resting on the gold dagger-hilt slung alongside his belt. He stamped his boots free of icy mud-clumps, then nodded to her and Valeria. "I looked inside the wagon earlier. The worst of the fire wasn't near the stove. Evidently an oil lamp shattered on the floor in front of the doorway and somehow caught fire. If you'd been sleeping inside, you wouldn't have survived—you'd have been trapped unless you woke in time and escaped through the flames."

The fire had started near the doorway? From a broken oil lamp? How? "All my lamps were metal and suspended on hooks from the roof. We never took them down. Furthermore, no one lit lamps there last night."

Valeria whispered, "Then this was either mischief gone horribly wrong, or the fire was deliberately set. I hope the arsonist didn't believe you were asleep inside. Bless the Eternal you weren't!"

Nodding agreement, Valo hugged Eliya, his voice lowered and rough. "I could have lost you! What would I have told Father?"

That she'd been murdered. Eliya leaned against her brother's shoulder, swallowing hard. "Who wants me dead? Valo, no sneaking thief carries a lamp. Didn't the prophets say that evil deeds are done in darkness?"

Valo's grip tightened. "I'll find the arsonist and kill him."

A quiet, authoritatively feminine voice lifted behind them. "Perhaps I was the target."

Torena stepped nearer, hugging her treasured Rone'en protectively. "My beliefs aren't exactly popular. And now that they're known, I might be targeted the farther north we travel."

"Or east," Valeria added, gloom weighing her words. "Ceyphraland's becoming equally hateful toward the old faith."

Eliya straightened. "An attack on my teacher is an attack on me."

"Nevertheless," Torena persisted, "my point is that if I'm a danger to you, I'll leave."

"No." Eliya rested one hand on her teacher's arm. "You made a pledge to my lord-father and you should be allowed to fulfill your work. I won't allow you to be hounded—if you're the true target. I'm not convinced you are."

Valo grimaced. "Whatever the motive, it's all the same to me. Whoever did this must be found and prosecuted for endangering you."

Lifting her chin, Valeria said, "The culprit will be found—my uncle and cousin are furious, fearing blame."

At once, Valo's voice and expression softened. "We don't blame them, lady. Or Belvasae. It's likely some maddened reprobate with an unreasonable grudge."

Eliya glanced from her brother to Valeria. Was she wrong, imagining admiration between these two? If not—

A man's bootsteps crunched over thin patches of early-morning ice. Adalric of Rhyve approached, perfectly groomed, swathed in a vibrant crimson cloak opulently lined and edged with ermine, his expression mingling sympathy and admiration. He clasped Eliya's hand. "How glad we are that you've escaped harm. If anything had happened to you, lady, Ceyphraland's losses would have been as immeasurable as Khelqua's. Believe me when I say that we're concerned for your safety and determined to bring the miscreant to justice."

He wove his gloved fingers into Eliya's, smiling down at her as if they'd been friends for years. His fondness for continuously holding her hand was becoming unnerving. Was he seriously pursuing her?

The northern realms wouldn't be pleased.

Valeria gave her cousin a teasing shove. "Are you trying to steal my friend? Go away."

"What if I do want to steal her? Why should she have to put up with Trisguard's bitter cold lands and citizens—and I won't even mention Rakiar."

While Valo frowned at Adalric of Rhyve's presumption, Aniketos of Ceyphraland stomped from his glorious tent toward the burned wagon.

His mouth set tight and grimly small, his gaze wide, stilled, and visibly shocked, Aniketos studied the sadly tilted remains of Eliya's once-beautiful miniature residence, then shook his head and called out, "Unacceptable!"

Eliya coughed, muting a bleak chuckle. She bowed her head in greeting as Aniketos stalked toward her, his black cloak flaring. "I woke from my nap, hoping I'd only dreamed of the fire. Whoever did this, when we catch him, I'll throttle him myself!" He halted in front of Eliya and puffed out an offended, mist-heavy breath. "What a blessing from the heavens that you slept in the ladies' tent last night."

Adalric groused, "I'm glad *you* knew she wasn't there, my lord. My heart near-stopped when I saw that wagon ablaze in the dark."

"Of course I knew!" Aniketos snuffed vigorously. "Obviously, her would-be assassin didn't—and I thank the Eternal for it!"

Adalric patted Eliya's hand. "As do we all. But Valeria should have mentioned ..."

His royal father cut off the genial complaint with a chopping wave. "The ladies' sleeping arrangements are no concern of yours, my boy. Blast that arsonist to the lowest gullets of perdition to be consumed with all cowardly scum!" He looked over Eliya's head and smiled a determinedly polite-host welcome. "Here comes Belkrates with that little son of his. He should send the boy away to a warrior's camp and toughen him up—the first ill wind will blow away that stripling and no one will remember he ever lived."

Belkrates nodded to them all, then deftly edged Adalric of Rhyve away from Eliya as if he were a fly and Eliya were a coveted dish at a feast. "Lady, my guards vow to me that they saw and heard no one last night—I questioned them all."

Young Belkian sidled around his father and—not looking at Eliya—observed, "I'd wager someone saw something and is afraid to talk. Or were paid to be silent. Or *made* silent. Has anyone searched for bodies?"

Valo leaned into the conversation. "My men searched the camp and found no bodies nor apparent traitors. Why don't we all hunt farther afield?"

Belkian hushed. But the tetrarchs of the south and the east sent guards to scour the lands directly around the camp a second time for any evidence of murder or other treachery. Something Lord-king

Danek and his Walhaisii had done just after dawn—before they rode off, searching for malefactors.

Had they returned from their foray?

Eliya looked across the camp at Danek's tent. One guard returned her gaze, waiting alone and watching in silence as he'd done since dawn.

❊

FROWNING, DANEK GLANCED over his shoulder at the small river valley. Had he heard a horse's distant whicker? The liquid rush of a stream flooded with snow-melt obscured too many noises. Not his favored way to hunt escaped menaces. But he and his men were in unfamiliar territory and the horses had needed water.

Riding beside Danek, Sion eased his patient golden horse's reins, then peered at the hillsides above as if he also sensed an enemy's nearness. "My lord, as the Eternal Liege lives, I'd vow we're being watched and followed."

"I agree. Let's ride up out of this gorge and claim the high ground."

They urged their horses to climb toward the afternoon sun, and the encampment. This morning's hunt had garnered no meat for his men, and no evidences that might lead them to the Lady Eliya's would-be assassin. What a cruel death the wretch intended for her! To be burned alive, helplessly trapped in her regal little traveling wagon with its near-useless high windows.

Mercifully, he'd seen the ladies trooping off together last night into Lady Valeria's tent. As it was, he'd been troubled ever since the blaze was vanquished, unable to sleep—unlike Aniketos and Belkrates and their heirs, who'd returned to their tents afterward.

Why would someone want Eliya dead? If only he'd a prophet to consult. To his Creator, he near-whispered, "Eternal, reveal the truth. Show me Your will!"

As they wound their way upslope through a copse of pale birch trees to the crest above the river, Danek ordered Sion, "Tonight, when we return, I want you and your most trusted closed-mouthed friends to listen for gossip while you're among the other guards."

Sion nodded. "We might have to share food with Ceyphraland's men. Too bad we don't have something substantial to cook. A buck, a boar, or at least a hare."

"Sion, you claim to be my cousin. You'll find something."

"Let it be as you've foretold! We'll prove prophets still exist."

Danek exhaled and grinned. "I was just wishing we'd a prophet to consult."

"See there? We think so much alike that you know it's true. We're cousins."

Danek's amusement faded as soon as they reached the crest and he glanced down into the valley. A small procession of guardsmen entered the area he and his men had just abandoned near the river, their gold coats and green badges announcing their allegiance to Trisguard.

They spied Danek, no doubt mistaking him for some minor and rustic lord out on a hunt with his men. As Trisguard's men eyed him, their commander lifted one hand and halted their procession. To reassure the undoubtedly tense detachment of men, Danek offered them a brief nod and a salute.

The commander returned his nod, then guided his men up the slope. Sion grumbled to Danek, "Why are they riding up to meet us? They'll delay us, and who wants to meddle with yet another realm? I'd prefer my late noon meal, and thanks!"

"Let's wait and learn their mission." Turning, he commanded his men quietly, "Don't tell them who I am, unless they're seeking the tetrarchs who accosted us."

Sion nodded and several men murmured, "Yes, my lord."

Trisguard's men rode up the slope, their horses slowed by the incline's rocky instability—a difficulty they could have avoided by threading their way among the trees, which offered a more gradual angle. Perhaps the Trisguard commander's thoughts were more straightforward than the average Walhaisii's. Sion muttered, "Their horses would've been better-off climbing the slope among the trees. By the Eternal's pity, I hope we don't see any of their creatures go down."

The commander reached the upper slopes first and rode to greet Danek. "Sir. I'm Keparos, fourth in command for our lord, Laros Rakiar of Trisguard. You're indigenous here. Have you seen an imperial encampment?"

"We were returning to the encampment—we left it this morning."

Commander Keparos grinned, revealing a chipped tooth. "A failed hunt, eh?"

"We've not given up yet." Danek smiled. "What brings you into Ceyphraland?"

"Seeking information for our Lord-king Rakiar. He's loath to leave his own lands without knowing the purpose of the imperial gathering."

Undoubtedly, Laros Rakiar feared an attack. Perhaps with justification. The attending tetrarchs and their heirs hadn't spoken of him directly, but whenever Eliya mentioned her imminent wedding, regal disfavor met her words amid icy silence.

At the very least, the tetrarch of the north would face severe censure for negotiating marriage to Eliya without unanimous imperial approval. Danek almost looked forward to the confrontation—except that Eliya might indirectly share the censure and be forced to accept blame.

By now, Commander Keparos' men had coaxed their bedraggled horses up the rugged slope with no lives lost, and they formed ranks behind their commander, awaiting orders. Danek studied his men, then paused, noticing one disturbingly familiar face.

Khelqua's upstart commander, Aretes, who'd insulted the revered Lady Torena in the Walhaisii highlands.

The man stared at Danek as if he'd met his doom. But his unnerved expression swiftly vanished, and haughtiness settled into its habitual lines on his harsh face. Danek nodded to him, then said to Commander

Keparos. "Commander, my men and I rode this morning to search for
... a malefactor who vanished from the imperial encampment. I am
Danek of the Walhaisii. I've pledged to Tetrarch Rodiades of Khelqua,
that we would safely escort his elder daughter through Walhaisii lands
to meet her future husband. Our journey's been troubled since its third
day. And—to be blunt—one of the troubles now waits among your
subordinates behind you. He's known to us as Aretes, third commander
in Ariym. Why is he among your men?"

The commander's grin vanished, replaced by wary, yet
commendable calm. "He's here because our Lord-king Rakiar placed
him under my command last night." Lowering his voice, Keparos
admitted, "I'm warned to not trust him, my lord, but to watch and
judge his behavior."

"Fair enough." Danek nodded. "May I speak to him?"

"Within my hearing, yes." Keparos raised one hand and his voice.
"Pledge Aretes, ride forward and speak to us."

His expression shuttered, Aretes rode forward, then held his horse
back slightly as if debating whether or not to flee. But any man with
sense would realize that flight invited pursuit, perhaps involving
arrows. Aretes halted his horse alongside Keparos', one pace behind
him to signify his subordinate status. Defiance twisted one corner of
the man's mouth as he greeted Danek. "Lord-king Danek of the
Walhaisii. I hope my presence here is not offensive, but I had no
choice."

"No choice?" Danek stared the man through. If only he could sift
this man's soul and find his true purpose. "Why do you—a commander
in Ariym's own royal guard—serve another tetrarch?"

Keparos twitched visibly, and his horse sidestepped as if sensing its
rider's distress. Aretes glanced at Keparos, then returned his attention
to Danek. Toneless, his eyes shadowed with exhaustion, Aretes said,
"I've no country left to serve, Lord-king Danek. I'm also tasked by my

new lord-king to tell Lady Eliya what she least wishes to hear: Ariym's drowned. Khelqua's no more."

Chapter 6

Wrapping her winter cloak snugly around her black gown, Eliya sat beside Torena on a pallet and peeked at her revered teacher's plain-bound copy of the Rone'en. While Valeria and the other ladies in the tent rested and listened to one of the maids picking out an idle tune on a harp, she ought to at least study. Still reading, Torena eased the book toward Eliya, allowing her to read the verses.

'... *But even if you suffer for doing right, you are blessed. Don't be afraid or worry about your enemies' threats. Instead bless the Liege, our Eternal Lord, in your hearts.*'

The words shone at her, the verses vibrant on the page as the Liege's Spirit beckoned, alive to her as never before. She could almost hear His otherworld whisper calling her from a timeless realm, "Walk with me! Be My Servant."

If only she could. What would it be like to simply walk away into a wilderness and survive from day to day, depending on Him as if she were some ancient prophet? In Spirit, she smiled, imagining simply running away from Trisguard. Yet, perhaps she could serve Him just as well, if not better, from her own intended place. Eliya leaned against her teacher's shoulder and whispered, "How do you always know the precise verses I need to read?"

"I don't." Torena traced the edge of a page, her touch as light and gentle as her whispered reply. "He's the Author, is he not? He knew the very words you needed to read today. Lady..." She hesitated, then looked Eliya in the eyes. "If the perpetrator who set the fire is found, I must be forgiving and plead for mercy toward him."

"What if others aren't inclined to be forgiving? Every man in the camp today intends to kill the offender on sight."

"Which is why I'm asking you, Lady Eliya, to support my wish for forgiveness if I'm the cause of last night's fire."

"But what if it was an accident caused by, say ... some drunken prankster. Or someone who hates *me*?"

"Drunken pranksters would have been found. And, who could hate you, lady? I've never heard so much as a whisper against you during all my years in the palace."

Eliya smiled. "I'd like to believe no one's despised me as a useless royal."

"I believe that's true. But if I say more, it'll sound like disloyalty to your royal family."

Her family. Straightening, Eliya gazed up at the tent's exquisite pierced bronze main cupola, which supported a matched pierced bronze lantern suspended above their heads. Soon, the messengers would return, wouldn't they? She'd hear that Iscah, Jesca, and Father were all well. Grieving, but well. Dear and blessed Liege, let it be so!

A hunting horn's distant call filtered into the tent, warning them of approaching visitors. Had Lord-king Danek returned?

The other ladies sat up on their respective pallets, smoothing their gowns and veils. Straightening and stretching on her thickly padded pallet, Valeria yawned. "Lady Eliya, if Lord-king Danek's returned, we ought to go greet him and see if he's captured the scoundrel who set fire to your beautiful wagon."

"Perhaps my brother's men are reporting to us after spying out Ariym. They should be here any day."

Valeria's silvery eyes shone at her reference to Valo. Clearly, Valo was a pleasing topic. Valo *was* handsome and gracious—in most circumstances. Eliya hid a smile and waited for Valeria's ladies to fasten her mantle. Would a match occur between Ceyphraland and Khelqua after all?

If so, her brother might live near Trisguard, and she'd have a sister-in-law's company during festival celebrations between the realms. Truly, she was allowing her imagination to run ahead of reality. She must settle into Trisguard first.

Horses' hooves and resounding huffs echoed through the encampment as Eliya stepped outside the tent with Valeria, followed by Torena and other highborn ladies of Ceyphraland's royal court.

Her breath misting, Eliya eyed the procession, then swallowed as her gaze swept from Lord-king Danek's handsome enigmatic face toward the men following him—some wearing gold tunics and surcoats.

Why had men from Trisguard followed Lord-king Danek into the encampment? Was Laros Rakiar hidden among them? Such things had been known to happen. Early histories of the empire often described rulers as so eager to meet their wives before the final vows that they resorted to disguising themselves and hurrying ahead of their own cavalcades.

Eliya almost shook her head. Not one man among these husky warriors matched the envoy's description of Laros Rakiar's long, elegant frame, graceful manner, and his richly curled dark ash hair. However ....

The formerly antagonistic Aretes caught Eliya's stare, then looked away.

Torena stepped up behind Eliya, her voice troubled, though she whispered. "Why is former commander Aretes riding among Trisguard's men?"

Eliya's thoughts fragmented, then regathered as she watched Aretes dismount. As any Ariym guard, Aretes had pledged lifelong loyalty to Khelqua. Either he was a traitor and a spy, or ... he'd found worse.

She swallowed as an unformed thought gnawed at the edge of her mind.

Before Trisguard's retinue halted, Valo hurried over to Eliya. "That's Aretes. Why is he here? I thought he'd returned to Ariym."

The dark, unwelcomed thought nagged again. Eliya looked up at her brother.

Valo averted his eyes and hushed.

❋

AWARE OF NUMEROUS PRYING stares focused on them, Danek fought dread as he, his men, and Keparos' retinue rode into the encampment.

Eliya must be told the truth, of course. Yet perhaps she'd already admitted to herself in her innermost soul that Khelqua had been swept away, with only handfuls of survivors scattered here and there across the empire. She was no fool. Nor was Valo, despite his green years, as the Walhaisii would say.

An obliterated Khelqua left nothing to Eliya and Valo but their royal blood, which now meant pitiably little to the empire's remaining tetrarchs.

Danek wasn't about to tell them so.

Let Aretes fulfill Rakiar's command. But why had Aretes told Laros Rakiar first? Where were the other men who'd been sent out the morning after the quakes and flood? Had they stayed with Laros Rakiar to serve the northern realm? If they were lost, then why hadn't Aretes done the honorable thing and sought out Valo first? As Rodiades only surviving son, Valo ruled any remaining scraps of land in Khelqua's foothills and highlands.

Danek dismounted, then eyed Aretes. Trust that errant commander? Not for a single breath.

His steps measured, dignified, Aretes approached Eliya and her brother. Danek drew near, watching, listening with all his might. To his credit, Aretes' naturally truculent expression faded and weakened, becoming somber distress. By the time he knelt before Khelqua's last surviving royals, Aretes fought visible tears, obviously too choked by emotions to speak.

As Ariym's former third commander struggled for words, Aniketos, Belkrates, and both their heirs marched toward Eliya, apparently to greet the Trisguard delegation and to provoke a confrontation. His cloak flaring in the cool air, Danek hurried to meet them. Young Belkian of Belvasae, and Ceyphraland's Adalric might have been twins, giving him identical glances of annoyance as he approached.

Whatever game Ceyphraland and Belvasae intended to play against Trisguard, it must wait.

Danek halted Aniketos and Belkrates with a harsh whisper. "My lords, please delay formalities. They've unwelcomed news."

✷

ELIYA GRIPPED VALO'S arm, then held her breath, waiting for Aretes to speak. She'd never seen a soldier so close to tears—a man preparing to describe incalculable destruction.

At last, his voice tense, subdued, Valo commanded Aretes, "Tell us your news."

Aretes removed his helmet and lowered his sweat-plastered head almost to the ground. "My lord, and Princess Eliyana ... our guardsmen were lost to a flood. And Ariym's submerged." Drawing in a deep, broken breath, the commander added, "From the hillsides above, I saw crests of towers but no life. For all—our guardsmen and Khelqua—the tide was too deep. Too swift to escape."

Father. Jesca, and Iscah ... dead. Eliya's stomach hollowed, plummeting with her soul as if she'd been dropped into a void—an eternal pit from which she'd never escape. Aretes lifted his head and looked up at her as if certain of retribution. Her tears reduced Aretes to a glittering, grief-blurred illusion, and her knees weakened, refusing to hold her.

Kneeling, she dug her fingers into the cold, sparse-grassed soil and held tight as she cried. Valo knelt beside her, one arm around her as he muted sobs, his body shaken by tears.

✷

NIGHTFALL'S COLD AIR soothed Eliya's tear-ravaged face as she stepped outside the ladies' tent. Valeria followed, clad in dark clothes, her sad eyes conveying sympathy. "I'll walk with you."

"Thank you."

Torena shadowed them, her swollen-eyed gaze distant as she hugged her copy of the Rone'en beneath her dark cloak. She'd said almost nothing today, but alternated between tears, silent prayers, and reading verses. Whatever the revered lady might think, Eliya didn't have the heart to question her. Torena might offer her more insights than she could accept this evening. Yet, Eliya had known the self-hidden truth. Now, to cope with undeniable loss, her mind offered the refuge of numbness. Pain from a distance.

As if discerning her mood, Valeria walked with her in commiserating silence. At last, she murmured, "I wonder how Lord-king Valo's doing."

Lord-king Valo. The very title acknowledged Father's death. Valo had grieved with her this morning, then isolated himself in his tent. She must check on him. They'd only each other.

Eliya drew in a shaking breath and released it. "Perhaps we should go find him and at least sit with him, even if he doesn't wish to talk."

Valeria sighed, her delicate profile and dark hair outlined against the deepening night, her voice wistful. "Exactly what I was thinking. I only wish I could do more for you both. And for your people. Perhaps the other tetrarchs might agree upon protections and help for Khelqua's survivors when they're found."

"We should urge Valo to request their assistance." Eliya fought for composure as her throat tightened around the words. "Khelqua's few survivors will most likely be found scattered throughout the highlands between the Walhaisii and ... the waters. Some of the Walhaisii are ... already searching."

She was going to cry again. How terrible to feel so helpless. A few more breaths eased her aching throat, but not the grief. Ahead, a cook-fire glowed, warm and inviting, with a number of the Walhaisii warriors seated around it, talking quietly as they waited for their evening pottage to finish cooking. Their leader, Sion of the Sevold Valley, bowed his head to Eliya as she and Valeria passed. One of his men began to hum a low, soul-haunting tune, which Sion and the others took up, adding their powerful voices to the music—the same lament they'd keened the evening they'd found the doomed Ceyphraland cavalcade. Were they lamenting Khelqua?

A chill ran up Eliya's arms.

Clearly summoned by the tune, Lord-king Danek stepped out of his tent, fastening his dark, fur-edged cloak. He looked toward Eliya. Then at his men.

She listened, wiping away tears as the Walhaisii crooned their dirge. Danek joined them, adding his low, full voice to theirs, the lament gaining force as their wordless plea lifted toward the skies, imploring the Eternal's compassion. Valeria rested one hand on Eliya's shoulder and waited with her, eyes closed as if praying while listening.

When the lament ended, Eliya murmured to Valeria, "I should speak to Lord-king Danek. I promise, I'll return."

"If I see Valo, I'll tell him what we've discussed."

Would Valo welcome Valeria's support? She was obviously infatuated with him, and making excuses to talk. Just as Eliya needed to talk with Danek. Soon, the whole encampment would notice and gossip.

Yet she needed to be near Danek, even if he said nothing. And he seemed to hope she'd talk with him. He waited, watching her approach, with Torena following several steps behind. "Lady, the Walhaisii grieve with you." His voice soothed gently, as if she were an orphaned child who'd wrung his heart. "You're not alone. As the Eternal Liege lives, I promise, whatever happens, you and your brother have friends among the Walhaisii."

"Valo and I thank you. I ... suspected the worst. But I hoped to be wrong."

"As did I." He turned, subtly urging her to walk with him. "My people will continue to search the waters' edges for survivors, I've no doubt. Anyone who's seen the destruction and remained unmoved is an unnatural being."

His quiet compassion, strength, and pledged support, heartened her. "Thank you. You've offered before I could ask."

"As I should. As we should."

Her next prayer should remain silent. She shouldn't even whisper ... "I pray Trisguard and its king are your equal."

A wry smile twisted Danek's full, handsomely curved mouth. "He will undoubtedly vow that he's more than my equal."

But would such a vow be true? Laros Rakiar hadn't met her hopes thus far—he'd only added to her fears. Meanwhile, she was staring at the Walhaisii's lord-king as if no other man existed. Undoubtedly, Torena would notice. Looking away, Eliya released a pent-up breath. "I mustn't linger. Perhaps tomorrow, my future husband will arrive." She rubbed one hand over her face and shook off a shiver. "I wonder what he'll think. Yet, everything's wrong. I'm a mourner going to my wedding feast, and I've nothing to offer. Merely a woman with no wealth, no country ... wrung-out and ghastly."

"No," he muttered, his voice so low she almost didn't hear. "Beautiful and courageous." His grumbled argument poured verses into those three words. His bleak parting glance added more—removing all doubt. He loved her.

She studied his eyes as they reflected the nearby fire, then silently bowed her head and returned to Torena, who waited, still clasping the Rone'en beneath her cloak. For the first time since this morning, when former Third-commander Aretes broke the devastating news, Torena's distress vanished. Just long enough for her to scold beneath her breath.

"Lady, others might wonder, but I *know* what I see when you two speak to each other. I beg you to maintain distance from temptation."

"I will. After I'm married and in Trisguard, I'll never see him again." What an unbearable thought. Every light in the encampment hazed and sparkled through unshed tears as Eliya fought heartache. She blinked, then turned away, but Torena turned alongside her, to walk with her.

And to take the arrow that shot toward Eliya from the darkness.

Chapter 7

Seated on the ground in the darkness near a tent, Danek grimaced. He was a fool to watch Eliya from the shadows, admiring the exquisite outline of her face, her ever-present regal composure, not to mention those occasional alluring hints of curves beneath her cloak. He'd surrender his personal fortune gladly if their situation could be changed. If only he'd ruled Trisguard instead of the Walhaisii. Or if she'd been some lesser-born lady he could have married. Instead, he must remain at an unbearable distance, watching as she and Torena turned away.

A thin creak and a whisper of sound caught at Danek's senses. Before he could spy the noise's source, an arrow hit with a low, resounding thud, just below the level of Torena's heart as she turned—a direct strike through her cloak.

Eliya screamed as Torena staggered. But when Eliya caught her teacher, Torena broke the arrow's shaft from her mantle, then revealed her beloved Rone'en, pierced by the arrowhead. She'd survived. Yet someone meant that strike to be lethal. Danek bellowed a battle cry to his men. "Walhaisii!"

His men set aside their evening meals and ran to join him, their weapons clattering in the darkness. Sion reached him first, his bearded face alight at the prospect of a chase. Danek motioned in the direction of the would-be killer.

A horse whickered in the gloom beyond. An unseen man's footfalls sped in the horse's direction, whipping through aged grass, crunching over twice frozen patches of snow. Danek charged at the noise.

Sion followed, his breath gusting, his weapons clattering against his belt—the muted noises echoed by all the Walhaisii following in the dark, hunting their prey.

❋

ELIYA ALL BUT DRAGGED Torena to the nearest fire—stepping around the Walhaisii's abandoned tin bowls of simmered grains and dried meat. "You're sure you're not wounded?"

"The Rone'en took my wound. Thank the Eternal!" Torena sat down before Eliya could coerce her, and she lifted one stern eyebrow. "Lady Eliyana of Ariym and Khelqua ..."

Her full name. Torena's next words would be death-serious. Eliya winced. "What? Tell me."

"That arrow was meant for you. Only an instant before—when the bowman took aim—you were his target. I'm sure I stepped into your place as the arrow took flight."

Eliya stilled as the realization sank in. Someone truly wanted her to die. Worse .... "Then the fire was set for me as well. And the cad didn't care that you and Vaiya would have died with me."

A man's voice called to her, "Lady Eliyana!" Aretes rushed toward her, wildly disheveled in a loose tunic and cloak, like a man shaken from sleep. Gasping as if panic had stolen his breath, he knelt at her feet and opened his bare hands, subjecting himself to her judgment. "My men told me that you ... and revered Torena were attacked. By the Eternal ... I had nothing to do with this! I told Lord Valo. He's coming."

Even as Aretes spoke, Valo and Valeria hurried toward the Walhaisii fire. Valo's golden eyes reflected fear within the flickering light as he studied Eliya. "Are you hurt?"

Valeria edged into their conversation, clasping Valo's hand and Eliya's arm. "Another attack? Eliya, we must find the felon—hunt him as he's hunting you!"

"Lord-king Danek and his men are chasing the man—they've a strong guess as to his whereabouts." Lifting her free hand, Eliya motioned to Torena, who was staring at Aretes. "The Rone'en took her wound. Symbolic, don't you agree?"

Valo made an impatient face. "Let's not talk theologies right now. Aretes, what can you tell me of this attack?"

The tousled Aretes insisted, "As the Liege lives, I had nothing to do with this. I wish no ill toward the Lady Eliyana. Nor you, my lord, nor the Lady Torena."

Valo shook his head. "What if I don't believe you?"

"Sir, it's true!" Aretes turned his hands palms up, bared toward Valo. "Kill me if you must, but believe me, it's true!"

Her face austere, formidable in the firelight, Torena said, "I believe you, commander. But now you pledge by the name of the Liege, whom you previously scorned. Why?"

Resting his hands on his tunic-draped knees, Aretes lowered his gaze and confessed. "Years ago, I laughed at the Liege's prophecy—that Ariym would be swept away, joining Khelqua's fate. And now it's happened as He foretold and as you believed. I was wrong and He has been like a searing bolt, burning my conscience as I sped here from Khelqua."

Eliya lowered her hand to make the humbled former commander look her in the eyes. "Yet you told Laros Rakiar first and you appeared among his men, wearing his colors, not Khelqua's. Why?"

"I rode day and night to reach the meeting place at the agreed time. I arrived last night, late. You weren't there. His men were, and they insisted I must speak to Rakiar. *He* insisted I wear his colors and pledge loyalty to him, reasoning that I no longer had a lord to serve. I was one man, lady, and they were many."

His tone distant, Valo asked, "What did Laros Rakiar say when you told him Khelqua was drowned?"

"He said nothing, my lord. It was impossible to read his face. He remained silent and walked away. I regret my pledge to him, my lord-king. I serve you."

Valo's expression hardened. "Do *not* call me lord-king! We can't be certain my lord-father's dead, therefore I refuse the title."

"Yes, my lord." But Aretes' voice betrayed his conviction. Rodiades, tetrarch of Khelqua, had died with Ariym.

A fresh wave of grief reduced Eliya to silence. But around the encampment, torches and lamps blazed to life, and Belvasae's servants called out in the night, heralding their lord-king's royal presence as Belkrates and his guards stormed through the shadowed encampment toward Eliya and Valo.

Eliya caught her breath, then rushed to meet the approaching horde, turning them away from the Walhaisii encampment to protect the abandoned dishes of food.

She'd no way to repay the Walhaisii, except to be sure they'd eat tonight.

※

STRAINING TO SEE AMID the moonlight's meager glow, Danek raced toward the noises and shadows of the errant man and waiting horse. Eliya's would-be killer vaulted into his saddle. Sion pitched a stone at the felon's silhouetted back. The stone thudded against its target, then struck the horse, which reared in the gloom. Unseated, the dark-cloaked man hit the ground and cried out, then shrieked beneath his panicked horse's hooves. Danek dragged his quarry away, while Sion's men crooned to the horse, then soothed it to a standstill.

Clearly lacking his mount's sense, the rider kicked, clawed, and snarled at Danek, "Release me, or I'll kill you!"

Danek cuffed the man, flung him to the ground, then stomped a booted foot onto his chest. "I doubt it."

While his captive wheezed for breath, the Walhaisii grappled with each other like hounds tussling to reach their game. Danek stepped back. "Strip him of his cloak and boots and all weapons. Don't kill him."

Sion said, "If you'd stomped him any harder, my lord, you'd have done the work yourself. Is he still breathing?"

Obviously fighting to answer, the captive sucked in a thin, reedy breath, then grunted unintelligibly dark words.

They bound the man, slung him over his horse and returned to the encampment. In the firelight's glow, Danek grasped the offender's dark, tangled, odiferous hair, then raised the man's head to glare into his face.

Into the eyes of the man they'd seized near the ambushed cavalcade.

"You soulless worm!" Danek wrenched the man off the horse and let him fall to the ground. "Obviously, you don't have enough skill to survive your work. Why are you stalking Khelqua's princess? Do you really want to die?"

His dark eyes glittering savage malice, the captive snarled, "What does it matter? We lowborn are a mere breath—you highborn are living lies."

Torena stepped into the light and gazed down at the man, her pale face and calm voice catching everyone's attention. "Is that reason enough to kill my lady? She's an exceptional young woman who'd listen to your complaints and resolve any with merit. Why kill her, after you've pledged she'd be safe?"

"I lied. No highborn are ever good! You're all corrupted!"

Accompanied by Valo, and the Lady Valeria, Eliya approached. Calm as if attending some courtly function, she knelt beside her failed assassin. "Obviously my death is vital to you. I'm sorry you've been given reason to think all highborn are corrupt. If I've ever done you harm ... tell me how, so I may beg forgiveness."

The man turned his face away, as if he couldn't bear to meet her gaze.

Why? And his expression ... furious yet laced with guilt. Danek growled to his men, "Search him, and his horse."

❊

ELIYA STOOD AS LORD-king Aniketos approached, closely followed by Adalric, their mantles' gold-embroidered edges gleaming and flashing in the firelight. Danek and his Walhaisii stepped back, allowing Ceyphraland's ruler entry into their circle.

Aniketos stared down at the prisoner, then looked from Eliya and Valo to Danek. "Has he talked?"

Valo grimaced. "Only to call us living lies. It's clear he meant to kill Eliya. But if he hates highborn so much, then we've more tempting targets around this encampment. Why kill my sister?"

Adalric leaned over the grimly-silent prisoner, then nudged him with a booted toe. "Is he sane?"

Torena answered, her teacher's voice mostly neutral—but carrying the slightest shade of compassion. "Not if he harbors such unreasoning hatred for all highborn. Someone's served him a near-lethal dose of poisonous injustice."

Gazing down at the man, Eliya saw his eyes widen, then turn disinterested once more, as if Torena had guessed a truth he must conceal. What had the man suffered at the hands of some nobleman, to foment such hatred? Was this her life's appointed task? To overturn injustices inflicted upon the powerless?

Danek's men returned and placed the man's saddle and gear at the Walhaisii lord-king's feet. Sion said, "We found nothing to hint at who he is or where he's from. His horse is unmarked, his clothes are a mix of Ceyphraland and Trisguard, like a man who's been crossing borders for years."

"Or," Danek added, "stealing from hapless citizens after he kills them."

Again, Adalric nudged his boot into the prisoner's belly, making the man glare. "What's the best way to get such a beast to talk?"

Eliya waved off Adalric. "Don't shame him, sir! I want to hear his story!"

Adalric chuckled and shook his head, but he stepped back. Though Valo stared as if Eliya had finally gone mad. "His story? He can tell any lie he wants! I wouldn't believe his least syllable!"

The prisoner grunted out a laugh, then looked up at Valo, irony twisting his thin lips amid his rough-whiskered face. "No? Well, believe this: Guard her!"

Valo flinched as if struck, then dove for the man, grasping his clothes just beneath his chin, shaking him. "What do you know? Say the words before we start cutting them out of you, slice by slice!"

The man howled out a laugh—a savage's cackle. A raving fit of mirth against the jest of his life, ending with a choked sob. "You highborn! You highborn ...."

He turned silent, staring at their boots, until Aniketos ordered his heir and their men, "Take him to your fire and guard him until we can question him by daylight—don't beat or wound him, but don't let him sleep either." To Eliya and Valo, he said, "Come with me. We need to talk. Valeria, you too. And Lord-king Danek, since you've made yourself responsible for Khelqua's own."

They sat on low-folding seats in Ceyphraland's spacious tent. Aniketos offered bread and drinks then dismissed the servants with a silent wave. Glancing from left to right, as if certain lurkers were listening just outside his tent's makeshift canvas walls, Aniketos muttered, "Take no offense at what I'm about to say."

Seated between Valo and Valeria, Eliya inhaled, bracing herself. No one ever bade others to take no offense without giving offense. She flicked a glance at Lord-king Danek. He waited, his dark gaze impassive, his hands resting on his knees. But Valo tensed, and Valeria eyed her royal uncle warily.

Aniketos said, "Khelqua's gone. Therefore—"

Therefore, they were of no use to any country, politically or fiscally. Beyond doubt, Aniketos was about to tell her, politely, that Ceyphraland's heir would look elsewhere for a worthy and wealthy bride. Adalric hadn't courted her for love, any more than Laros of Trisguard had. Why should the northern king want her now?

Beside Eliya, Valo gripped his sword's decorative hilt, his tensed knuckles and fingers paling against the shimmering gold. "Therefore, my sister and I are now worthless to the Syvlande Empire."

As if relieved that someone else had voiced the dreaded words, Aniketos exhaled, then rubbed one hand over his face. "Just know that you're welcomed in Ceyphraland, if you're willing. Swear fealty to me and I'll grant you lands enough to comfortably support you and your progeny—and to provide a dowry for Eliya later, if anything should happen to Laros. But if Laros outlives you, Lady Eliya ..." he shrugged.

What had prompted his taciturn attitude toward Laros? Eliya tugged her mantle closer and murmured, "Sir, thank you for concerning yourself with our future. Tell me ... do you dislike my future husband?"

Ceyphraland's tetrarch frowned, compressing his full mouth, as if pondering his true feelings for Laros. At last, he said, "Laros Rakiar always keeps his word. We are polite to each other, yet he's not someone I would choose as a friend. He trusts few people. With reason. His father was a brutal ruler and parent. I didn't approve of how the elder Laros treated his family."

"That's more information than I've ever heard of him," Eliya admitted. "I've been told little except that he's regal, a fearless fighter, and a handsome man."

"True." Aniketos helped himself to some of the soft, salted bread left by the servants, then reached for his gilded silver cup. "He's more regal than I am. He bests my Adalric in most of their private archery contests, though Adalric always outlasts him in hunting, dancing, and eating. He guards his opinions, and—be warned, lady—he's sparing with gifts, unless he has reason to seek favor."

Mustering courtesy, Eliya smiled. "He sent impressive wedding gifts. However, those will return to Trisguard when we marry. *If* we marry. I did wish he would attempt to communicate with me more."

Valo leaned toward Eliya. "Do you have concerns?"

"None that matter. Father signed the contracts and, from what I've been told, I can't break the pending marriage. Nor can Laros. Unless I'm proved barren or I commit adultery."

"And what about him?" Valeria sniffed. "What if *he* commits adultery?" When her uncle lifted his grizzled royal eyebrows, visibly shocked at her question, she huffed, "Well? Sir, what if he does? Not that I've heard scandalous rumors, but how is such a contract fair toward any wife? Particularly a defenseless wife from some foreign land?"

"In theory," Valo muttered, "Khelqua's power would have restrained Laros and protected my sister."

Yet Khelqua was no more.

Into the bleak silence, Danek said, "We pray no such concerns blight the Lady Eliya's marriage." He eased his shoulders, then nodded toward Aniketos. "While we're all speaking freely, I'll ask—for my country's sake—what other reasons did you have for gathering here and waylaying the Lady Eliya's wedding cavalcade? Am I right to be suspicious of this meeting between three of the four tetrarchs?"

Aniketos waved aside Danek's concern. "The Walhaisii aren't our targets. However, Belkrates and Laros Rakiar ought to be present before we discuss our overriding concern—even above the suspiciously clandestine negotiations surrounding the Lady Eliya's marriage. Laros should have consulted us." His wearied gray eyes reflecting sadness, Aniketos studied Eliya and Valo. "You are both too young to be cast adrift amid the Syvlande's chaotic politics. Belkrates and I considered sending for your lord-father—how I wish we had!"

If they had, then Father might still be alive. Eliya clenched her hands together, fighting the impulse to berate Aniketos. To accuse him. And to cry.

Dry-voiced, Valo asked, "Why didn't you?"

"Because ..." Aniketos sighed, then began again. "We feared he'd believe we were accusing him, though we were not."

"Yet," Eliya said, "you would have accused Laros Rakiar."

"Not accuse. We wished to understand his motives for arranging his wedding so hastily and secretively."

Valo leaned forward, his golden eyes wide, his voice emphatic, its veneer of courtesy thinning further. "Last year, my lord-father wrote to Ceyphraland and Belvasae, requesting suggestions for my sister's marriage prospects. Neither of you replied. What was he to think? How was this marriage contract secretive if Laros Rakiar was the only tetrarch to respond?"

"He wasn't the only one. As you now know, your lord-father never received our replies. Nor did our messengers return. What am *I* to think? You both saw my last cavalcade."

A shiver slid over Eliya's skin and prickled her scalp, almost feverishly intense. Had Laros Rakiar condemned that doomed cavalcade?

Sharp taps sounded against the tent's metal doorpost and Adalric called out, "My lord, your presence is required." Ceyphraland's heir swept inside, his dark cloak flowing back from his pale tunic, which was speckled with blood. As Eliya and the others stood, Adalric said, "Sir, one of Trisguard's men killed the prisoner lest he attack the Lady Eliya again."

Nausea threatened, forcing Eliya to swallow hard. A man had died because of her. Not for her, granted, but still ... because of her.

Rage reddened and mottled Aniket's blunt face. "A deliberate murder! Does he think himself judge above all? May the Eternal strike him if I don't! Where is he?"

Eliya followed as Aniketos stormed from the tent and snatched a javelin from one of his startled guards. Adalric hurried just behind his lord-father, whispering fiercely, "He was angry. He considered it a favor to Ceyphraland to kill one of the men who attacked the Princess Eliya and our cavalcade. Half our men agree with him, and the other half are undecided. Trisguard's men too, are debating the death. We require their good opinions if we're to win our purposes from this gathering!"

While they walked, Eliya followed, listening. Until Valo, Lord-king Danek, and Valeria closed ranks around her, suffocatingly near. She shoved gently at Valo. "Back off!"

He grasped her arm, his low and fierce. "You're the only family I have! Our prisoner spoke two true words: 'Guard her!' And so I shall. Two attacks on your life *are* enough, aren't they?"

Eliya's throat constricted, hurting too much to speak—almost too much to allow breath. As they walked onward, she gripped her brother's hand hard. Valeria attended her only one step behind. Beside her, Danek walked close as another brother. But when she finally looked up at him, his glance said far more.

Why couldn't he be Laros Rakiar?

She looked away, at torches and fires turned to wavering, glittering lights by the burning threat of tears. Blessed Eternal Liege ... how would this end?

Aniketos halted as a clutch of men dragged a captive toward him. They dropped the man at his feet. Ceyphraland's tetrarch snarled, "Who are you to defy my orders within my realm! Answer, sludge-gullet, before I stomp you flat!"

His nose bloodied, his lip split, the yellow-cloaked man lifted his voice just enough to be heard. "I'm Treven of Fieldsend in Trisguard. Forgive me, sire, I had no right to do what I did. But that man attacked my future queen! Not once, but twice from what I've heard. Who knows if there be others of his kind? I was angered beyond reason. Punish me as you please—I bow to you."

Aniketos backhanded Fieldsend's dark-matted scalp. "Don't bother bowing to me, wretch! You deserve the flesh slit from your muscles, and your offensive corpse shredded before it's tossed into a fire! Your air of humility reeks of arrogance—and I'd not trust you with cleaning up after my enemies' dogs!"

As Aniketos ranted, Eliya studied her supposed defender.

Treven of Fieldsend, who'd been so offended for her sake, and so willing to make an example of her failed killer, hadn't looked at her once. Obviously, he didn't give a copper-weight for her safety or good name—he'd wanted her attacker dead for another reason entirely. What had the prisoner known that must be kept secret?

And why would a man of Trisguard silence him?

Finished raving, Aniketos whacked the miscreant's ribs with the javelin's blunt end. "You will bury the man you murdered then hurry your sorry carcass out of my realm before I fling you into the grave myself! May the Soul Hunter blight your path and stalk you to death!"

As the man scuttled away, followed by Ceyphraland's guards, Valeria whispered, "He didn't once look at you."

"I noticed. And I wonder why."

※

THE SUN'S MIDDAY WARMTH mingled with birds' songs, beneath a cloudless, brilliant-blue sky.

Sheltered between Torena and Valeria during midday meal, and watched by Valo and Danek and their men, Eliya could almost imagine that last night's nightmare had been exactly that; a nightmare. Except that a heap of raw-damp soil rested over a grave just beyond the encampment. Once the tetrarchs finished their meeting, her murdered attacker would be left in this remote stretch of land, with no one to tend his resting place. She could almost see him standing near, as if still living, shaking his head, muttering, "You highborn! You highborn ..."

As Eliya dropped the last bite of herbed bread—too full to finish her meal—a flourish of hunting horns sounded from the opposite side of the camp, breaking the morning's superficial calm. Among the Trisguard faction, more hunting horns blared, as men shouted, "Lord-king Laros! All stand! Laros Rakiar of Trisguard!"

For an instant, Eliya stared at the tumult, her benumbed thoughts stumbling over themselves. Her future husband was about to enter the encampment.

And, mercy, he'd see her looking ghastly as any woman who'd suffered a terrible night's tears.

Followed by Valeria and Torena, she fled for Valeria's tent, to Vaiya's capable hands, praying as she ran.

Chapter 8

Valo called into the ladies tent a second time, a subtle edge to his sociable voice. "Eliya, are you perfect at last? Everyone awaits your glorious presence in the main tent."

Before Eliya could soothe him with a promise that she was almost ready—minus a few hairpins—Valeria called back, "My lord, if you're half as glorious as your sister, the empire will be blinded when you two walk in together. Have patience, good sir."

His patience obviously failing, Valo muttered, "Eternal, save us!"

As Vaiya hurriedly oiled Eliya's clean fingernails, Torena clasped Eliya's second-best gold-embroidered violet mantle around her shoulders, settling its shimmering collar to frame and reveal her bare throat. The instant Valeria's ladies slipped the last glittering pins into Eliya's upswept hair, Valeria herself stepped forward with a polished silver mirror for Eliya's inspection.

Her embroidered green gown, shimmering jewelry, and subdued face paints didn't conceal the distress reflected in her golden eyes. But what could Laros Rakiar expect? By now, he knew that her sadly diminished dowry—contained within three beautifully painted chests filled with shimmering garments, gems, and coins—couldn't match the extravagant sums her father had promised to deliver after the wedding. Her former wealth lay drowned in Khelqua.

She must not think of Khelqua. Of her family and Ariym lost forever.

Eliya lifted her gaze from the mirror to Valeria. "I'm ready. Thank you, everyone."

Valeria smiled, her silvery gaze wistful, as if she suspected Eliya's unexpressed grief. "You look perfect. If he's not thrilled, then run, because there's no pleasing him."

Eliya tweaked a long gold-adorned hair pin snugged uncomfortably close to her scalp. "I pray he's as gracious as you've been."

"If he's not, Ceyphraland will have much to say. My lord-uncle thinks you're delightful."

"Your lord-uncle is the delightful one. I've been nothing but a burden since my arrival."

Valeria snagged Eliya's arm, leading her toward the entryway. "Enough—you're not a burden. Your sorrow's speaking. Let's greet your betrothed and see if I'm right. You'll amaze everyone."

The instant they stepped outside, Valo met them, his golden eyes brightening, banishing his earlier impatience. "You both look wonderful." He led them toward the main tent, taking a muddied path heavily overladen with straw to protect their shoes and gowns. "Aniketos introduced me to Laros Rakiar." Valo grimaced at Eliya over his shoulder. "He's impressive, but deciphering him's the trouble. He might as well be a Chaplet guardian's statue."

Lovely. Eliya sighed. Just what every princess wanted to marry—a royal statue.

Prayers mingling with her fears, Eliya entered the main tent and blinked at the immediate hush. Was her appearance so ghastly? Danek's open admiration told her otherwise. Aniketos smiled as if he were a fond relative, and Belkrates nodded, visibly approving her, before giving Laros Rakiar a thinly veiled glance of annoyance. Standing between their royal fathers, the heirs, Adalric and Belkian, stared steadily at the northern tetrarch like hunters watching potential prey.

Adjacent to the tetrarchs and their mistrustful heirs, Trisguard's tall, elegant ruler waited at ease, clad in deep green edged with gold. His dark ash-brown hair and short, meticulously sculpted beard emphasized the slim, perfect lines of the most aristocratic face Eliya had ever seen. Laros Rakiar affected more hauteur than her brother Iscah, or even her lord-father.

His silver-gray eyes cool, he studied Eliya as if she were a landscape or an evening sky. She nodded toward him, maintaining dignity as she'd been trained, watching his face for clues to his true nature. She must find some way to love this man. Indeed, she must choose to love him, chilling demeanor notwithstanding—Torena would counsel her to remember her training and emulate her royal mother's graciousness and patience.

Laros Rakiar met her gaze and smiled. "You are more beautiful than my envoy described. I'm delighted to greet you at last." His smile didn't reach his fine gray eyes.

Suppressing a shiver, she matched his courtesy.

Lord-king Danek had shown more warmth at their introduction, despite his wariness while meeting her family in Ariym. Would Trisguard's lord-king remain a stranger? She must break past his cool façade.

"Thank you, my lord. I'm delighted to meet you as well. My lord-father regarded you so highly." Not as much as Belvasae's royal family, and certainly not as highly as Ceyphraland's but well-regarded insofar as Rodiades comprehended Trisguard's aloof tetrarch. "I hope your journey wasn't too inconvenient."

"Not inconvenient so much as unexpectedly extended." Rakiar bowed his head toward the elder tetrarchs. "I suppose this gathering was past due. If only Syvlande's western tetrarch could be here as well." His enigmatic gaze touched Eliya's again, then cut to Valo. "I've heard about Khelqua's tragedy. We regret your losses."

He might have been regretting a cup of spilled water instead of an entire nation swept away. How could he be so cold? Would he despise her grief? Eliya swallowed. "Thank you, my lord."

Valo nodded, his gaze and voice older, stern-edged. "Thank you. For your sake, my sister changed from her mourning."

"I appreciate the tribute." Laros Rakiar lifted Eliya's hand, placed it on his proffered arm, then looked toward the two elder tetrarchs and their heirs. "In honor of Khelqua, we should keep wedding festivities to a minimum. I have sent word to my court to cancel all large gatherings except the feast I've planned for my people in Iytair. We will observe a year of mourning. Meanwhile—"

"Meanwhile," Belkrates interposed, his tone vinegar-sharp, "Since you've arrived at last, Lord-king Laros, we can move our tents to fresh ground. I suggest we delay any talks or marriage celebrations until the task is complete."

Laros regarded Syvlande's southern tetrarch without a flicker of emotion. "Move? To where?"

"Four long furrows in any direction you please." Belkrates' small mouth turned sullen. "As long as it's fresh land. We've been in one place too long, and the dung heaps are becoming mountains outside the camp."

Aniketos nodded. "Agreed. Otherwise, the air will be foul when the weather warms, which I hope will be soon."

Laros shrugged. "If you deem the matter imperative, we'll move. But if you move north, go no farther east. There've been night hound sightings this past week in the Na'Khesh foothills, and gauatchens aren't creatures to be trifled with."

"Then," Belkrates sighed, seeming bored, "We'll move directly north, four long furrows."

Valeria stepped toward them, entering the conversation. "Forgive me, my lords, but ..." She faced Laros. "The Na'Khesh foothills? Your people are certain they've seen night hounds in the borders of my lands?"

Rakiar stared at Valeria as if he'd never seen her before. As if she might be almost fascinating. "That's true. Your lands border on Trisguard's. I'd almost forgotten. Yes, beware, lady. If the famed gauatchen doesn't stalk your people after dusk, then a na'khesh might at dawn."

She stepped away, as if Rakiar were a monster disguised as a man. But Adalric of Rhyve nodded toward Laros, changing the subject. "Cousin, I believe you owe me another round of archery."

"Later, perhaps." Rakiar's finely curved upper lip twitched as if he were almost amused. "But I should think that you're still stinging from your last defeat."

"No." Adalric grinned. "Only plotting revenge."

"Very well. A wager?"

Ceyphraland's heir shook his head. "I can't afford your wagers, lord-king."

"Because you realize defeat's inevitable," Rakiar taunted. He clasped Eliya's hand, then leaned down to murmur, "Lady Eliyana, let's walk while the encampment's taken down."

Without so much as a nod or parting pleasantry to anyone else in the tent, Laros Rakiar, ruler of the northern realms, led Eliya toward the tent's entryway. Just before Rakiar stepped outside, Eliya looked over her shoulder, expressing her silent dismay to Valo, and Valeria.

Aniketos and Belkrates both stood, their outrage raw and undisguised at being snubbed.

Why was she worried? Rakiar's rudeness wasn't hers. Eliya gathered her skirts, one-handed, to protect them during their proposed walk. Rakiar tugged her outside, complaining, "You are too slow, lady."

"Your legs are longer than mine, my lord, but I'll hurry." She quickened her pace, consigning the hems of her richly embroidered garments to their fate amid the mud and straw. "Tell me of the gauatchen—the night hounds. Are they fierce creatures?"

"Ravening. Forever hunting food, no matter what species that food might be."

"In other words, human flesh is also their prey."

He faced her, his smile again adding no luster or life to his gaze. "Yes. And while we're discussing hunted creatures, my men tell me that you've suffered two attempts on your life."

"The most recent was an arrow aimed at me. Torena, my revered teacher, caught the arrow instead."

"Was hers the grave I saw on the camp's edge?"

"No. She survived—the arrow embedded itself in a book she was carrying. That grave belongs to my poor attacker. He was assassinated last night, by one of your own men."

"Ah. I'll question my men later. What happened the time before? Obviously, another failure."

Another failure? She looked up at him from beneath her lashes. Had he hoped for success?

His mask-like expression revealed nothing. Perhaps he'd wanted her dead and counted the 'failures' as disasters. She pressed her fingers into his arm, feeling muscles, long and lean beneath the richly embroidered dark green sleeve as she guided him toward the charred remains of her once-beautiful wagon. "The time before, someone threw incendiaries into the wagon my lord-father commissioned for this journey. The fire was set during the night when we were all asleep. Thankfully, Lady Valeria had invited me to stay the night with her ladies in her tent."

Rakiar studied the charred, now collapsed remains of Eliya's wagon, which still rested in the slightly muddied area not far from Valeria's tent. He nudged one booted toe at a crumbling, fire-warped board, his words toneless. "You would have died had you been asleep inside."

She could read anything into his voice. Submerged horror. Muted dismay. Or a near-buried wish that she'd actually died amid that fire. How could he be so neutral?

She looked up at him, trying to gauge his temperament. Movement, at the edge of her vision, made her turn. Valeria, Torena, and the other ladies neared—all preoccupied with keeping their flowing garments away from muddied ground, when they weren't eyeing Rakiar with appalled fascination. He *had* been rude. Yet he was stunning to behold, his thick ash-dark hair gleaming in the sunlight, while his well-fitted garments commanded notice of his tall, lean, regal body. Some might argue he was more handsome than Danek. Yet good looks meant little without kindness.

If only he'd possessed a tenth of Lord-king Danek's warmth and humor. As it was, she could only hope she was wrong, and that he didn't long for her death.

Eliya gathered her courage. "My lord-king. We both know Khelqua is ... gone ... and I've almost no power or wealth to offer you and your people. Do you wish to escape our marriage contract?"

"Escape the contract?" His gray, unblinking gaze held hers. For an instant, an errant gleam hinted his temptation at her suggestion. But then he shook his head. "No. I'm a man of my word. Trisguard won't break the contract."

Why not? The words were on her lips until she realized that Valeria was watching closely. Eliya smiled and nodded to her cautious highborn hostess.

As if making up her determined mind, Valeria smiled and approached. "Cousin Laros! Please forgive me—I didn't truly welcome you. Congratulations on your pending marriage by the way. Your bride is so lovely and well-respected, that I promise you are much-envied."

"Am I?" Bland interest flickered across his handsome, beard-accentuated face. "By whom?"

"Oh, any of the lord-kings and their heirs. Just look at them. They're regretting their slowness in writing to Khelqua for the Lady Eliya."

Another smile traced its way along Rakiar's face—a lazing smirk that sent alarms chasing over Eliya's arms, just before sweat chilled her flesh and made her exhale. Rakiar gloated. He didn't care about her, but oh, how he relished any small victory over his tetrarch peers. Obviously, they could all go hang themselves as far as Laros Rakiar was concerned. Even her.

How sad that he'd suffered a terrible childhood, with a brutal lord-king father. But why should she subject herself to its pitiless aftermath? She would not marry this man.

✸

HIDING HIS FISTS BENEATH his heavy cloak, Danek watched the obtuse northern tetrarch. How could Rakiar be such a fool? With or without her royal family and Khelqua's wealth, Eliya was a match for any lord-king of the Syvlande Empire. And this sneering over-dressed northerner couldn't be bothered to treat her with courtesy.

For no coin whatsoever—a service to all civilized people—Danek would knock Laros Rakiar unconscious and steal Eliya.

Bootsteps scuffed the straw beside him. Valo halted beside Danek and groused, "I was right from the very beginning! Rakiar should have fought for the privilege of marrying her."

Beneath his breath, Danek said, "I would have challenged him."

"I would have sharpened your weapons, then helped to bury him. I should just take her and escape. Before this meeting's over." Huffing his exasperation, Valo added, "That's another thing! Why are we here? Belvasae and Ceyphraland should state their purposes, resolve their differences with Rakiar, and we should all leave!"

"I hope it will prove that easy. This gathering of tetrarchs promises adversity—I trust none of them." As they talked, Danek watched another messenger ride into the encampment, dismount, then kneel before Belvasae's lord-king.

Ceyphraland's Lord-king Aniketos seemed unsurprised, and the two tetrarchs lingered near Belkrates' regal tent, their heads lowered like a pair of assassins, plotting their attack.

✸

A QUIET BREATH OF EVENING air caressed Eliya's face, then toyed with her hair while she, Valeria, and Torena stood on the fringes of Adalric and Rakiar's archery competition. Her guards from Khelqua, and Valeria's guards from Ceyphraland stood around them, almost blocking her view of the competition, and of Lord-king Belkrates' prized fresh ground.

He'd been right, of course. The previous encampment was too overrun, trampled and rimmed with waste pits, dung heaps, and a grave. Belkrates, seated on the other side of the current archery round, was now smiling—even nudging his glum heir with one royal elbow. Perhaps, if Belkrates was in a good mood, she could quietly persuade him, and Lord-king Aniketos, to forbid her marriage to Laros Rakiar. After all, the marriage contract *had* displeased the two tetrarchs.

Yet her marriage wasn't the true reason for this gathering of tetrarchs. Something else was afoot. The guards around her seemed restless, shifting and muttering dark comments among themselves, while casting suspicious looks toward other tetrarchs' factions.

As Eliya watched Belkrates and Aniketos, Valeria leaned toward her and whispered, "Well. What do you think of your future husband?"

Eliya shifted her gaze to Rakiar, who sauntered over to Adalric to change places in the current round. His elegant form drew whispered comments from the onlookers—not all of them complimentary. "He's rude. Cold and distant as a frozen mountaintop. I want to escape him."

"I think Valo agrees with you. Look at how he's folding his arms."

Valo's arms were indeed crossed, his stance hostile, his expression grim as he watched Rakiar raise his bow, anchor his shot, then release an arrow, which flew straight to the target-dummy's straw heart. As the arrow thudded home, Valo nodded to Danek.

While the crowd applauded, both men stalked over to Eliya and Valeria.

Eliya's guards stepped back, allowing Danek and Valo space. Valo leaned down, still grim, but a half-smile played over his face. "I see your guards are taking their job seriously."

"Yes. They're suspicious of all the new faces from Trisguard. Perhaps the murder and the assassination attempts have unsettled them."

Valo scowled. Lord-king Danek murmured, "I wish you blessings, lady. May your marriage bring you joy."

"It won't. Unless *he* is hiding a tender soul."

"Oh?" Valo lifted one dark eyebrow, his golden eyes glittering, intense. "You don't like him then?"

"No. And he's not interested in me. Only in his own glory."

"That was my impression too."

Danek muted a cough—covering a disdainful laugh. "We're in agreement, then. Can you break your contract?"

Valo nudged Eliya and muttered, "Father gave me a copy of the contract. I'll read it tonight and look for an escape clause."

Eliya stared at her brother. "Would you?"

"Do you approve?"

"Yes."

"Then I will." Valo tilted his head toward Rakiar. "The thought of feasting with that pompous crown-stand during holidays will put me off my food indefinitely."

Twice more, Laros Rakiar sent arrows straight to the hapless target, widening the hole over the dummy's straw heart. The onlookers applauded politely. Their applause increased as Adalric marched forward, obviously fighting for the grace to concede defeat once again.

Danek half-bowed, including Eliya, Valo, Valeria, and the ladies in one sweeping glance. "Forgive me."

He left them, his powerful warrior's grace blending admirably with his regal stride. When he chose to don the aura of a lord-king of the Syvlande Empire, albeit a minor lord-king, everyone gave way to

Danek. Each man in his path retreated, bowed, or half-bowed to him, depending on rank. Even Laros Rakiar allowed him a polite nod, his false smile broadening as he listened to Danek's hushed request.

Whatever, Lord-king Danek asked, it amused the tetrarch of the northern realms. Adalric shrugged, then grinned and handed Danek a quiver of arrows and one of Ceyphraland's gleaming pale bows.

Danek gathered a clutch of arrows from the quiver, clasping them easily, the feathered fletchings dangling beneath his strong, sinewy fingers. A secretive smile played over his features, drawing Eliya's appreciation despite Torena's subtle nudge. Never mind that Torena watched him as well—everyone did, and with reason.

Of all the lord-kings, he remained the most intriguing.

Danek's strong features smoothed, then his gaze narrowed, focused on the straw dummy. He set one arrow's nock against the bowstring while three remained dangling between his fingers. Before Eliya caught and released a full breath, Danek shot four arrows in rapid succession, ferociously surrounding and trapping Rakiar's two much-applauded arrows in the dummy's straw heart.

As the Ceyphralanders and Belvasae's citizens cheered and the Trisguard men howled Danek's feat, Eliya's troops and Danek's applauded and whooped like packs of jubilant boys, hammering each other's shoulders and backs with their fists.

Amid the uproar, Danek nodded politely to Rakiar and Adalric, obviously thanking them as he returned the bow.

Rakiar smiled and nodded, his face mask-like. But an instant later, he eyed the arrow-bristled target again, glowering before he turned away.

❋

HER GAZE FIXED UPON the distant, glittering stars amid the violet-blue night sky, Eliya sat on covered haybales between Valeria and Torena, enjoying their camaraderie, as well as the flickering hearth before the women's tent. Low-voiced and wary, Torena read from the journey-rumpled, arrow-pierced Rone'en at Valeria's earnest request. "*Seek the Eternal's sanctuary. For even surpassing the strength of the mighty aeryon, His wings offer you shelter.*

His truth shields you and His might is your stronghold.

Dread flees Him. The night's terrors dare not approach,

nor will you fear the arrow strike ....'"

Eliya leaned against her revered teacher and muttered, "Last night, you were reading the Histories and Praises. Why war songs tonight?"

"Considering everything that's happened, I feel the verse is appropriate—an impression, somehow. I've been praying today—I'm uneasy."

"I've been uneasy as well. Tomorrow, we'll know the true purpose of this gathering. Now that *he* is here."

"And here he is indeed." Valeria straightened, looking toward Laros Rakiar, who strode into their circle and glanced around, handsome, perfectly groomed, and seeming bored. His gaze rested on Eliya and he lifted one eyebrow.

As he approached, she stood with Valeria. Torena closed her book, then retreated, clearly ceding to Rakiar her place beside Eliya. Of course, he took Torena's seat as his due. But then he pulled the Rone'en from Torena's hands as he settled onto the leather-covered hay-bale. "What are you three reading?"

"The Holy Verses." Eliya's heart thudded an extra beat of agitation as Rakiar fanned through the final pages pertaining to the Liege.

He glared up at Torena, offended as if she'd spit on him. "The Rone'en. This book's fit only for hearing while translated by priests. Why did Rodiades allow you to teach her such upstart beliefs?"

Rakiar threw Torena's Rone'en into the fire, the flames gusting around the illuminated pages as the book landed.

While her attendants gasped and protested, Eliya dove after the Rone'en, snatching the ruffled pages before they caught flames. "Sir, this book's an ancient treasure!"

"Ancient?" He huffed his outrage as Eliya thumped the book onto bare soil and pounded out the sparks flaring around it. "Not the final testimonies—they defy ancient traditions."

"They complete ancient accounts, my lord. If ..." Eliya's protest faded beneath his unrelenting stare. Rakiar's cool, steadfast gaze promised that if she said more, she'd never be forgiven. Was winning an argument worth sundering their marriage before it began? Not that she intended to marry him.

Yet, escaping this betrothal undoubtedly required discretion to save his limitless pride, and ensure her safety.

Rakiar lowered his chin, exactly as he'd done when Danek bested him during the archery round. "Lady Eliyana, throughout my life, every person who should have owed me loyalty has betrayed me. Am I to count you among those traitors?"

Her mouth dried. Would he dispose of her with false charges of treason? In the past hundred years, Several of the Syvlande Empire's queens had been executed on lesser charges. Two were northern queens. Eliya controlled herself. "I'm loyal to those I love—my future husband in particular, my lord."

"Your revered teacher will not bring her dogma into my realms. My subjects and I won't endure it."

"Yes, my lord. We'll heed your advice."

He left the communal fire, his deep cloak flaring as he stalked away.

Eliya exhaled, then traded looks with Torena. "I'd never suspected he was religious."

"*That*," Torena said, "is why so many mortals love the Chaplet faith—they live worldly lives and buy forfeits to earn eternity, without consulting the Eternal." Torena clutched Eliya's hand, her own fingers cold. "We won't be safe in Trisguard."

"If I have my say, dear Torena, we won't go to Trisguard."

"You won't have say," Valeria hissed, "Because I won't allow Trisguard to have you!"

✻

WAKEFUL AFTER A TOO-restless sleep, Eliya softly pushed aside her thick layers of coverlets, crawled out of her pallet, then crept from the ladies' tent, sweeping her cloak around herself as she stepped into the chilly dawn air.

Muted clatterings caught her attention from the south, then from the east, where multitudes of shadows shifted about the camp.

Soldiers. Hundreds of soldiers. From Ceyphraland and Belvasae.

All armed for war.

Chapter 9

Valeria confessed as she and Eliya slowly walked through the encampment, followed by Torena and by Valeria's ladies. "Yes, I knew of the armies. Your unapproved impending marriage was the perfect excuse for my uncle and Lord-king Belkrates to force Lord-king Laros into this meeting."

"Why?"

"We'll be told at the meeting."

"And my lord-father wasn't summoned to this meeting because—?"

"I don't know. I presume because he would have defended your marriage and Rakiar."

Eliya huffed out a maddened breath. She must fight bitterness. If her lord-father had been invited to this enclave, as he should have been, he and her siblings might have survived Khelqua's catastrophe. Bracing herself against the pain, Eliya nodded. What else could she do? Except hope that good might come from this meeting. "Then this gathering might yet dissolve my marriage contract. I pray it's so! I'd rather live in a mud hut and forage a wilderness for the remainder of my life than marry Laros Rakiar."

Valeria answered with a mirthless chuckle. "My lord-uncle would be offended at the idea of allowing a princess to live in poverty. We need only be patient to achieve our goals."

"And what are your goals?"

"Peace and happiness, of course." Her silvery eyes shining in the morning light, Valeria whispered, "I hope you approve. I intend to beg my lord-uncle to offer Lord Valo a contract. For me."

Valeria of Ceyphraland ... her future sister-in-law? As the thought took hold, Eliya smiled. "Of course, I approve—*if* Valo approves, and if you have your lord-uncle's permission."

"He's granted me the freedom to choose my husband as long as he approves of the man personally, and as long as I marry a highborn lord. Valo fulfills both requirements. Even better, I won't have to leave Ceyphraland. My lord-uncle has feared I'd fall madly in love with some foreign-born lord and ...." Her voice trailed off as Lord-king Laros Rakiar crossed their path, then waved back his guards and halted, his gold-embroidered green robes splendid, glittering and refracting the morning sunlight.

Rakiar waited, silently commanding their approach. Eliya marched toward him with Valeria gripping her elbow as if prepared to drag Eliya away should their confrontation turn violent. Rakiar didn't smile, but his gaze flicked from Eliya to Valeria as if comparing them. Eliya bowed her head toward him. "Good morning, my lord."

Valeria forced a smile. "My lord-cousin. Good morning."

Rakiar's fine mouth thinned slightly, though Eliya couldn't decipher his look. A suppressed smile? Annoyance held at bay? The ruler of the northern realms released a breath. "Why do you call me 'cousin', lady? The term's a mere courtesy and hardly apt."

He was annoyed, then. Eliya held her peace as Valeria explained, cool and polite. "I call you cousin because my lord-uncle has named you one and I bow to his example."

"Don't." Again, he glanced from Eliya to Valeria, and his gaze rested on Valeria. "I wish you a good morning, ladies."

As he walked away, trailed by his guards, Valeria muttered to Eliya, "I don't want to be related to him anyway." She sniffed. "But why should he take offense at being called cousin? It's always been a pleasantry between the tetrarchs and their families. Anyway, I'm sure if we check our lineages, we are related somehow."

Watching her handsome, soon-to-be rejected fiancé, Eliya shrugged. "Perhaps he believes his dignity's lessened by such familiarity."

"Or ..." Torena ventured from her place just behind them, "Perhaps he doesn't wish any possible connections, however distant, to be remembered, lest his Chaplet faith forbid marriage to the Lady Valeria."

Valeria snorted. "That's ridiculous!"

Torena watched Laros Rakiar's tall form as he walked away with his guards. "Lady Eliyana, what if he's already planning your replacement if you should die early? My contention's possible. He said almost nothing to you just now, as if you no longer exist for him. It seems he considers Ceyphraland's Lady Valeria a finer option."

Valeria put one hand to her throat. "You're serious. You're convinced he's considering me? No! Not for ten thousand shieldcoins. Thank the Eternal that my lord-uncle loathes his royal 'cousin'!"

"Only consider the thought." Torena leaned toward them, her voice low. "How easy it would be for a tetrarch of the northern realm to be rid of his wife. Childbirth. An accident during a journey. Or ... an agreement. Some of the Chaplet 'faithful' are eager to forgive even a murder if the guilty one forfeits a fabulous amount of gold to the Chaplet's ruling council."

Childbirth or an accident. Or a secret agreement to have her murdered. Eliya almost nodded. A man like Laros Rakiar would pay the forfeits and never think of her again. Unless he relished cruelties and savored memories of her death.

A young man bellowed from across the encampment, "Lady Eliya!"

Valo. As Eliya met her brother's gaze, he lifted a scrolled parchment, then stalked toward her, his dark mantle flaring, quite befitting his grim gaze. Beside her, Valeria breathed, "Isn't he beautiful? I could stare at him forever."

"I'll tell him you said so."

Still gazing at Valo, Valeria whispered, "Say also that I'll marry him as soon as possible. Thwarting any of the northern realm's plans will be his wedding gift to me."

Valo stopped and grimly offered Eliya the scrolled parchment. "Your marriage contract, sister. Have you read it?"

"Some, before Father signed it. But that was months ago. What's wrong?"

"If Laros Rakiar repudiates the contract, he will owe you most of his personal income for years to come. *Sixty thousand* gold shieldcoins. Lord-king Danek estimates that's more than five years' worth of Rakiar's household revenues."

"Therefore, Rakiar must marry me."

"He has no choice. Unless he's willing to carve his own meat and groom his horses for the rest of his life."

"Yet, once we marry, he can do with me as he pleases. What will happen if I refuse?"

A wry grimace worked one corner of Valo's mouth. "Father will owe him an equal amount."

"But," Eliya persisted, "father's no longer here. Nor is Khelqua. What will *I* owe him?"

Valeria murmured, "Nothing. You didn't sign the contract. Any court in Ceyphraland will absolve you." With a tiny cough, she added, "Uncle will be sure of it."

"Lady Valeria...." Valo's golden eyes glinted, alight with admiration. "If I didn't already adore you, I would now."

Pretending irritation, Eliya waved a hand between them to break their mutually appreciative looks. "Obviously, you're both lovestruck. I order you two to plead with Lord-king Aniketos for a marriage contract. Immediately."

"Thank you." Valeria rested one hand on Valo's arm. "If my Lord Valo doesn't object, I'll kneel before my uncle at once."

"I'll kneel with you," Valo pledged. He glanced over his shoulder, adding, "After we've heard whatever Lord-king Danek has to say."

Danek? Eliya schooled her expression to serenity, then risked glancing at the Syvlande Empire's most fascinating lord-king, who approached at his typical brisk pace.

His strong face calm but warmed by the morning's light Danek nodded to them. "Lord Valo. Ladies, good morning. Lady Valeria, I've no wish to cause you trouble, but this should be presented at the meeting today." He removed an arrow from beneath his cloak and offered it to Valeria. "A reminder. This arrow was taken from one of the bodies in the ambushed Ceyphraland cavalcade. Their lives should not be forgotten. The arrow's yew wood, taken from the Na'Khesh Mountains, perhaps bought from your own people, then used against them."

Her silvery eyes darkening, Valeria lifted the yew arrow from his hands. "Thank you, my lord. We intend to speak to my lord-uncle at once—before he's too distracted by today's meeting. Will you walk with us?"

She nodded to Valo and they walked ahead, leaving Eliya with Danek. He smiled down at her, "Shall we follow them, lady?"

Aware of Torena watching her sharp-eyed as a silvered, ever-hovering Aeryon, Eliya said, "I wish we could claim their same purpose for walking together."

"What purpose, lady?"

She smiled, drawing her mantle closer as she walked with him, following her brother and Valeria.

※

LISTENING TO VALO AND Valeria as they knelt before Aniketos and requested royal blessings and a marriage contract, Danek cut a glance toward the Lady Eliya.

She wished to claim their same purpose. With him.

Eternal Liege .... She was serious. The melancholy look on her face told all as Aniketos laughed and held out his broad hands to Valo and Valeria ... then hugged them together, approving their union. Eliya envied their joy, even as she smiled at her just-betrothed brother.

He must consider the implications for his people. He'd ensure the Walhaisii never suffered retribution from Trisguard if ... no, *when* he broke Eliya's marriage contract. Unless she broke the contract first.

What was she planning?

❈

TRAILED BY HER GUARDS, Eliya walked with Torena to Valeria's tent. Just beyond the encampment's fringes, two armies waited. Trisguard's much smaller force waited near the designated meeting area, notably restless. What were they planning? Eliya murmured to her teacher, "I'll be grateful to have this meeting done. Not even Valeria knows why the tetrarchs have congregated here. My marriage contract's been a superficial excuse for this meeting. If these lord-kings can't reach an agreement, we'll be thrown into war here and now. By gathering in one place, they've all put themselves in danger."

"I believe it's providential." Torena sighed. "I'm sure the lord-kings trust they prompted this meeting, but undoubtedly the Eternal's willed them to act upon His plans."

"And what might those plans be?"

Torena's gaze turned distant. "As much as I dislike the thought .... If the whole empire's become as faithless toward the Eternal's Rone'en as Khelqua and the northern realms, what should the Eternal do, except ruin the Syvlande?"

"If that's so, then I pray we survive its ruin."

In Valeria's tent, Eliya washed her hands and face, then allowed Vaiya to dress her and pin up her hair. "A diadem, lady?"

"Whatever you please, Vaiya. I trust your judgment." Would this be the last time Vaiya dressed her? Would Laros Rakiar insist upon marrying her and taking her away—to kill her in the northern wilderness before dawn? Or would he whisk her to the northern realms, then put her to trial and death for trusting the Rone'en? Or would he ensure she somehow died of *natural* causes? Enough women died in childbirth—perhaps he hoped she would.

She mustn't allow her imagination free rein. Her thoughts behaved as untamed horses trampling reason, urging her to panic.

Willing herself to relax, she prayed inwardly as Torena fastened her ceremonial cloak while reciting low-voiced from the Rone'en.

"*Whom shall we trust?*

Wickedness burns like a fire; consuming briers and thorns.

Tempest and ruin,

Battle and dirge

Why should the faithful be crushed?

Shout to the Eternal, who will destroy your conqueror!

Seize your weapons and lift your shields."

Eliya smiled. "Revered Torena, that's a very warlike set of verses. What are you saying?"

Her dark eyes fierce, Torena met Eliya's gaze, unflinching. "I'll accompany you to this meeting."

"You won't." Softening her tone, Eliya added, "I command you to stay here and pray for us all. Whatever happens, I want you to live and protect the Rone'en and Vaiya. Go to the Walhaisii. Of all the lands, it seems they've welcomed the Liege's believers. You won't be safe anywhere else."

Vaiya begged, "Don't speak as if you'll die, lady."

"Vaiya, I'm about to openly reject the Lord-king Laros Rakiar. Whether I marry him or not, I may have no choice about dying."

Her hands shaking, Vaiya pinned Eliya's exquisite pearl and amethyst diadem high in her hair, then fastened Eliya's matching pins to her purple and gold ceremonial cloak. Finished, she pressed Eliya's shoulders as if to reassure them both. "Who could think of hurting you? Lady, you've never looked more beautiful."

"Good." She'd never felt readier to take up weapons and go to war.

She stepped out of the tent just as Valeria and her ladies trooped in to dress for the meeting. Whether or not they'd be allowed to attend, clearly, they'd honor this event's potential significance with their richest garments. Her eyes shining like polished moonstones, Valeria seized Eliya's hands and kissed her cheek. "You look magnificent! Rakiar will rue what he's lost—the fool! Wait for me and I'll walk with you."

Torena edged her way outside and stood with Eliya. "At least I can wait and pray with you while you wait for the Lady Valeria."

Before they could clasp hands to pray, Aretes approached Eliya and bowed, one hand resting on the sword strapped to his side, the other flexed uneasily around his official long-spear. "Lady, your lord-brother has pardoned my offenses and granted my plea to join his guards today. May I again beg your forgiveness and approval? And yours, Revered Torena?"

Eliya studied his trimmed hair and freshly scrubbed face. Aretes watched her, anxious as a man begging for his life's wish. "You'll defend a vanquished, sunken country? Why?"

"While you and your brother live, lady, something of Khelqua remains. Perhaps enough of our people survived the disaster to regroup and reclaim our country's borderlands. Who can say? As for the Tetrarch Laros ...." Aretes shook his head. "I cannot trust the man."

"What about Revered Torena and the Rone'en? If you despise them still, then I cannot trust you."

Muscles worked visibly beneath Aretes' dark-bearded jaw, a man struggling for composure. "Years ago, I told myself that the Liege's prophecy was nothing. I fed myself lies. Even so, the Rone'en is true—that sea of dead water testified against me."

Raw honesty played over his face and resonated in his voice—imploring the least chance to help restore his lost homeland and faith. Eliya nodded. "Thank you. I believe you. And I don't trust Rakiar. Guard my brother against him, please."

Aretes pressed a fist over his heart. "Lady, I'll join the others and guard you both."

Clad in a splendid crimson gown, Valeria emerged from her tent and brandished the arrow as if it were a sword. "I'm ready. My ladies will wait with Torena and Vaiya."

Valo approached, his dark robes almost obscuring the heavy gold baldric and sash over his sweeping purple tunic. "Not to rush you, ladies, but Lord-king Danek's already at the meeting place."

Eliya had no need to search for Danek. As they neared the meeting place—she heard his richly indignant voice lift over the press of the gathered crowd. "I have no army. Why should I send away my own guards?"

Rakiar's lordly voice answered, "One guard's sufficient for each dignitary, my lord. Any more and we'll be crowded out. Aren't we all among friends?"

Eliya and Valo grumbled in hushed unison, "No!"

Valeria laughed and swiped her arrow toward them. "Trust me, the Ceyphralanders will defend you three—you've our hearts. However ...." She paused at the edge of the circle of spring grass chosen for this meeting. "Rakiar has two guards. My lord-uncle and cousin each have one. Lord-king Belkrates and his heir have two ... and we'll each have one. Trisguard's outnumbered."

Valo hissed, "At least we haven't been disarmed!" He nodded to Aretes and another guard. "Aretes, stand with the Lady Eliya and let your comrade guard me. Where are our seats?"

While Valeria sped across the open grassy circle to sit near her lord-uncle and Adalric's regal chairs, Eliya nodded toward a pair of haybales covered with several layers of canvas and fine dark wool. "There. Near Lord-king Danek." Adjacent to Laros Rakiar—much too close—the four of them facing the delegations from Ceyphraland and Belvasae.

His movement languid, Belkrates lifted one hand from his chair's arm-rest, summoning a Chaplet cleric to pray. Coughs and shuffling stirred the crowd of onlookers, as did a cool springtime breeze, making Eliya shiver.

Aniketos began the talks by snatching and raising Valeria's yew arrow to gather everyone's attention. "Before we address the main topic, I wish to say that the next time my people are attacked, as they were at the borders between Ceyphraland, Trisguard, and the Walhaisii, I will search out the offenders and strike them all down, no matter who they are! Fair warning to all offenders!"

His tone lazy, almost disinterested, Laros protested, "What's a rogue-bandit's attack to do with anything of importance? Speak of imperial business. I wish to know why you've dragged me here, away from my wedding preparations."

As if he cared. Eliya suppressed a snort.

Adalric straightened on his covered haybale, obviously infuriated. "The 'rogue-bandit's attack' is important to us, cousin. Some of Ceyphraland's finest statesmen, clerks, and guards died while traveling imperial roads, though they should have been safe! This matter certainly pertains to imperial business. If these had been Trisguard's citizens, you would have been hunting for offenders and demanding recompense."

"However—" Rakiar leaned forward, his voice oozing genial sarcasm. "This doesn't explain why you've disrupted my wedding plans."

Clipping every syllable to a sharp edge, Valo called out, "There will be no wedding! Khelqua is gone, and I see no reason for my sister to marry a man who treats her with such disrespect."

Laros Rakiar dismissed Valo's accusation with a scornful wave. "That's your own misperception. I have never disrespected the Lady Eliyana, and I honor my contracts."

Eliyana leaned forward, coercing him to pay attention. "*I* signed no contract, Lord-king Rakiar, and I've no interest in a connection I'm not bound to honor. There's no profit in the marriage for either of us—I've no wish to marry you."

"Furthermore, Cousin Laros," Aniketos brandished the arrow, arguing loudly, "We've all found it interesting that only *your* messengers arrived safely in Khelqua to negotiate with Lord-king Rodiades after he sent us all requests to discuss his daughter's marriage prospects."

"Mere chance!" Rakiar sat back and folded his arms across his chest. "You were laggards, you and Belkrates."

"We were attacked!" Belkrates snapped. "Belvasae and Ceyphraland alike! Your negotiations and motives are suspect, because we've lost worthy citizens who never had a chance to defend themselves or to represent us in Khelqua. For the Lady Eliyana's sake, we declare the contract void. There will be no wedding!"

Standing in attendance around the royals, the courtiers hushed, clearly avid for their slightest reactions.

"Good!" Valo groused beneath his breath. Relief weakened Eliya almost to faintness.

"No matter." Laros Rakiar stretched out his long legs and relaxed, bland-faced. "I'll plan another."

Aniketos shrugged, then winked at Valeria, who smiled. Ignoring them, Rakiar continued, "Now that we've dispensed with nonessentials, tell me why *you two* dragged me here—to a meeting in the middle of nowhere."

Belkrates reached into an ornate box held by an attendant and lifted out a magnificent gold crown, its flaring spires and golden sapphires reflecting the sunlight. "We intend to dissolve the empire."

Disbelief silenced everyone for an instant. Then, as others around him either applauded politely or muttered disagreements, Rakiar protested, "I disagree!"

"Too late," Aniketos told him, as Adalric smirked. "We've already approved the dissolution."

Already approved? Eliya shook her head. *This* was why they hadn't invited Father to their meeting. Aniketos and Belkrates wanted Laros Rakiar and his forces overwhelmingly outnumbered, and Khelqua sidelined in order to coerce Trisguard's approval. She nudged Valo, who looked away, undoubtedly remembering their brother's grandiose empire-conquering plans in Khelqua.

His motions defiant, dramatic, Belkrates placed the magnificent sun crown at his booted feet, then stomped it flat, while the onlookers seethed with whispered comments and gasps. Belkrates said, "Did you think, Rakiar, that we'd wait, idly yawning, while Trisguard and Khelqua united to wrest control of the empire from us? No! We'll divide this crown into five pieces and return to our separate countries. Just as this crown was brought together by our separate realms, so shall it be broken."

Rakiar stared at the extraordinary crown's flattened remains, his handsome face blank, his voice smooth. "You cannot be serious."

"We are," Belkrates told him. "We've dissolved the Syvlande Empire. Our separate peoples want their freedom."

Rakiar's sculpted mouth twitched, his eyes widening in murderous feral outrage. A shiver ran down Eliya's back as Rakiar stood, baring his teeth as he snarled. "My people and I disagree!"

Lord-king Aniketos snapped, "*You* are outvoted!"

Valo stood, shielding Eliya while Rakiar swiped a dagger from his belt. "I cancel your votes!"

Chapter 10

Swift as a man who'd practiced, Rakiar swung the dagger toward Valo, drawing a crimson line over his throat, then turning the weapon away—to hurl it at Aniketos, embedding the blade solidly below his left shoulder.

Eliya and Valeria screamed. Every man within the meeting circle bellowed and grasped for weapons.

As Eliya fought to reach her brother, others gripped her arms—Danek and his cousin Sion. She struggled to shake them off. "My brother's wounded! Let go!"

But as Valo's guard dragged him away, Aretes lunged toward Rakiar, aiming his gleaming long-spear at the northern ruler's heart. Rakiar's two guards struck aside Aretes' spear, then stabbed him, toppling him dead into the grass before Eliya.

More onlookers charged into the circle, joining the fray—two noblemen clad in Trisguard's green hues lifting daggers toward Eliya. Undoubtedly, Rakiar had ordered her death. Danek stepped backward, shielding Eliya while Sion mirrored his movements from the opposite side, trapping her between them, echoing each other's war cries.

Eliya ducked out of their way, then planted her hands in the cold, coarse grass. Only fools risked attacking the Walhaisii king; he'd destroy them all. Yet, "Liege, save him! Protect Danek and Sion!" And Valo.

Was Valo dead? Danek and Sion held their ground, almost back to back as they defended her. One of her attackers fell at Danek's feet, his gray-green eyes going blank as he died—staring at her. Eliya flinched, then looked ahead. Her gaze fixed on Aretes' shimmering fallen spear. She must not think. Only act. Rakiar's polished black boots tramped along the grass just beyond Aretes' spear as Rakiar and his guards battled Aniketos' guards. By Rakiar's actions, he'd fight his way toward Belkrates and kill him.

No. Rakiar must not claim the sun crown.

Eliya scooted away from Danek and Sion, grabbed the spear with both hands, braced herself, then lunged upward at Rakiar with all her might. The spear slid beneath his embroidered cloak, then stopped with an appalling flesh-muted thump. Laros froze, his gray eyes widening in obvious pain. Eliya released the spear as Rakiar met her gaze.

Baring his teeth, Rakiar swung his sword downward at Eliya. Danek blocked the blade with the flat of his sword. Adalric charged Rakiar, screaming, "Murderer!"

Rakiar's sword clattered against Eliya's diadem-encircled head, then dropped to the grass. Danek lunged to shield Eliya, but Adalric collided with Laros Rakiar, knocked him flat, then stabbed him over and over, screaming in a berserker's unintelligible rage.

Sion and Ceyphraland's two guards subdued Rakiar's men. The tumult faded almost as swiftly as it had begun, leaving only the groans of wounded men, and blood seeping from the dead. Before Eliya could stand, Danek swung an arm around her and scooped her to her feet, almost carrying her toward Valo.

Ashen, held half-propped up by his guard, who was staunching his bloodied neck, Valo exhaled when he noticed Eliya. "I saw you go down. I thought you were dead."

"No, Danek and Sion sheltered me. Let me see your wound."

"Lady," the guard warned, "His throat's flayed. Not a pretty sight."

Ignoring the man, Eliya lifted the folds of yellow cloth—a cloak swiped or loaned from an onlooker. Beneath the woolen folds, Valo's throat oozed blood from beneath a wide flap of skin. His neck resembled a badly blundered shaving accident.

Danek leaned in and stared at the wound. "It's not pulsing blood. We'll steep him in wine and ale, then stitch him up. He'll live."

Eliya pressed the cloth down on her brother's wound, then kissed his cheek. "Obey Danek, please. I'm going to find Valeria."

She didn't mention Aniketos. But Valeria would be with her beloved lord-uncle.

A small hushed crowd encircled Aniketos. He lay, eyes closed, his head resting in Valeria's lap as she smoothed his hair and dripped tears onto his face. The bloodied lethal dagger rested at his side, near the crimson-spattered Adalric, who huddled beside his father's corpse and sobbed.

Eliya touched Valeria's shoulder making her look up.

Her reddened eyes streaming tears, Valeria pleaded, "Valo ...?"

"Lord-king Danek says he will live."

Valeria wept. After fighting to compose herself, she begged, "Stay with us, Eliya!"

"I will. For as long as I'm needed."

Torena's voice called across the crowd, "Lady! Eliya—"

Eliya stood. Torena rushed to her, snatched her into a fierce embrace worthy of any mother, then refused to let go.

✻

AS DUSK MERGED INTO night, Eliya folded her arms tight to suppress inward tremors, then stared up at the stars while Torena waited beside her.

They'd sent Rakiar's men north this afternoon, bearing his corpse, as well as one-fifth of the crushed sun crown, and the news that the Syvlande Empire was no more.

The grieving Adalric sat vigil over his father's body, while Valeria comforted herself by tending Valo's wound with remedies of gall, honey, and pulverized onions offered by her ladies.

As for tomorrow .... Eliya sighed. She'd be sure Third Commander Aretes received an honorable burial, his spear resting over his chest as befitting a high-ranking guardsman of Ariym and Khelqua.

0Had she dealt Laros Rakiar a death-blow with that spear? Or had the frenzied Adalric sent Rakiar onward? The guards were still debating who'd actually landed the killing wound.

Eliya said, "Torena, I believe I killed a man today. Tell me about the Eternal's forgiveness."

Torena shook her braid-wreathed head and stared up at the stars. "Why do you believe you need forgiveness? You defended others by killing Rakiar. Furthermore, Lord-king Rakiar also killed before he died, lady—with malicious intent."

"But my intents weren't altogether pure. Yes, I was truly frightened for everyone else he might kill, including myself. Yet I *wanted* him dead, particularly for wounding Valo. That needs forgiveness."

"Then ask the Eternal, lady, as the Liege bid you. But remember that the difference between your soul and Rakiar's is that his Chaplet faith required him to purchase his soul's eternal forgiveness with forfeits. Mortal gifts paid to mortal hands. Whereas you ...." Her gaze seeming enraptured, caught in the sparkling heavens above, Torena continued softly, "Through your faith and His love, the Liege purchased eternal forgiveness for you, with His immortal blood. No mortal can buy such a priceless gift." Shifting her gaze from the stars, Torena smiled. "I pray you rest easy tonight."

"I pray so too."

Several pairs of footsteps approached. Lord-king Belkrates, Belkian, and Danek. Eliya forced herself to not stare at Danek. To not run to him and hide her face in his chest. But perhaps then, she'd stop shivering.

He watched her steadily as if gauging her mood. But he remained silent. Lord-king Belkrates spoke first, almost unforgivably serene despite today's carnage. "Did you notice, lady, that the attempts on your life ended when Laros Rakiar entered the encampment? It was as if he'd ordered the assassins to stop."

Hadn't Belkrates heard of the two men who'd tried to kill her amid the fray? Eliya nodded. "Thank you for declaring the contract void, my lord."

"Of course. From the moment I heard of it, I suspected he'd conspired against us all. Aniketos believed Rakiar would attempt to make himself emperor of the Syvlandes, supported by Khelqua's wealth. Therefore, we decided to break the empire. It was already splintered. We no longer follow the old ways and old beliefs. The prophets, if they ever existed, belong to ages past. Our people are clamoring for their freedom and identities as separate countries once again."

"They'll buy their immortal souls from mortal hands," Eliya murmured.

"What was that, lady?" Belkrates stepped nearer.

"A thought, my lord. Nothing you'd consider sensible."

Belkrates shrugged. "What will you do now, lady?"

She smiled, deliberately casual. "I'll remain with the Lady Valeria until my brother's fully recovered. Then ... I'll return to Khelqua's borders. If any of my people have survived, I must find them. Beyond that, I don't know."

"You will always be welcomed with kindness in Belvasae. We honor your courage."

"Thank you, my lord. I'll remember your generous offer." Yet, he'd abandon generosity if he knew she trusted the Liege's Rone'en. All of Belvasae might assemble to watch her die at Belkrates' command.

Obviously considering his duty done, Belkrates bowed and departed with Belkian, who followed him like a bored puppy.

Lord-king Danek remained. "I'm proud of you—spearing Rakiar as you did." He hesitated, then asked, "How long will you remain in the west?"

"How long will I be welcomed in your realm of thorns, my lord?"

"Forever. If you choose." His dark, quiet gaze promised refuge.

Too tired to care if anyone might be shocked, she stepped into his arms and rested her face against his chest.

Danek folded his cloak-covered arms around her, holding her warm and close, as if welcoming her home.

✾

HIS EYES STINGING WITH the overabundance of burning incense clouding each smoky street corner, Danek walked one step ahead of Valo and Eliyana as they followed Aniketos' silent funeral procession through Ceyphraland's crowded, shrine-filled capitol of Rhyvemuth. The city reeked of Chaplet worship rites, and the citizens stared at him as if he'd been dragged from the savage wilds of a distant continent. As he lived, he'd never return to this place. Unless Eliyana required visits with Valo.

For her, he would endure even Rhyvemuth's sweltering, stone-cobbled streets, and Ceyphraland's rank foods. But not for too long, he hoped.

Their pace measured and somber, they followed Aniketos' embalmed gold-draped body as it was carried reverently along the main thoroughfare and into one of the most imposing buildings within the city—a towering, spire-spiked stone crown of a temple. A place so choked with incense smoke that Danek held his breath as Aniketos was laid to rest within a marble coffin, while Adalric, king of Ceyphraland watched in silent grief.

Valeria, stately, somber, and draped in black, placed white flowers within the coffin, then stepped away. Toward Valo, who'd exchanged vows with her five nights past, sharing Danek and Eliyana's quiet marriage ceremony.

As Valeria retreated, Adalric stepped forward and offered his father a final gift—Ceyphraland's crushed, sparkling portion of the Syvlande Empire's broken sun crown.

The symbol of Ceyphraland's freedom, won at Aniketos' death.

❋

VALO RESTED HIS WRITING quill in its tray and smiled at his wife as she swept into their shared writing room, then closed the door. How could she be so beautiful? From the first instant he'd seen Valeria, she'd been 'the delight of his eyes', to quote a verse from Torena's Rone'en.

And Torena thought he hadn't paid attention to her during lessons. Who would guess that he'd miss his revered teacher and her stern gaze? Almost as much as he missed Eliya, now traveling west with Danek and Torena.

Valeria wrinkled her delicate nose, teasing, "We've been in residence only one day, my lord, and you're already writing to your sister?"

"Yes." Valo tugged his wife closer, his senses exulting as she bent and kissed him.

But then she slipped from his grasp. Valo huffed. "Wait! What are you doing?"

"Sharing a secret."

As Valo watched, he rubbed his scar, which itched his neck furiously, though it was healing. Valeria unlocked a covered shelf on the far wall and eased open its carved wooden door—the hinges squealing their thirst for oil. Smiling, Valeria tugged a heavy book off the shelf and placed it on the table before him, almost creasing his note to Eliya. He set aside his writing, then opened the book.

Illuminations, brilliant with thick black lines, vivid crimsons, bold blues, greens and gold paints. And verses, so familiar they stole Valo's breath with the homesickness of reading them. He might still be sitting in Torena's writing room, facing those words. "The Rone'en."

"Yes. The Eternal's sacred Word. My family's copy, commissioned twenty years past." She smoothed a page tenderly as if it were a child's cheek. "We've kept it secret. Some factions at court consider it

dangerous to hold, much less interpret without training. Too
controversial. Too biased against the beloved Saint Syphre and Saint
Gueron. Before he died, my lord-father said we should bequeath it to
a house of Religious, where it will be studied and protected. He feared
possession of the Rone'en would ultimately be outlawed, risking his
descendants' lives."

Did she expect him to part with this book so soon? Valo slid the
book away from her hands. "We can study and cherish it as mightily as
all the Religious in a single house."

"I was hoping you'd say so!" She laughed and sat in his lap, kissing
his bewhiskered face. "Read one chapter to me now, then I'll allow you
to finish your letters."

"Yes, lady." He nuzzled her soft face, then began to read.

❋

ELIYA FORCED HERSELF to look ahead. To face the
autumn-tinged landscape.

Three days past, they'd departed from Danek's rustic stone and
timber palace—a welcoming, yet imposing structure situated on a
shorn hill, surrounded by forests that scented the Walhaisii king's robes
and furs with the mingled fragrances of cedar oils and woodsmoke.

Even now, as Danek lifted Eliya from her horse, those delicious
cedar aromas tempted her to remain in his arms, never mind that
Torena and most of his household milled around them like a restless
colony of ants, setting up their encampment.

Danek kissed Eliya and rested his forehead against hers, their
unborn child shifting within their embrace. "Lady, I'll never
understand why you chose to marry me."

"I suspect it'll be useless to explain, except to say that I love you."

"Are you certain you want to face this?"

"Yes. But ... please, walk with me." They crossed the wide clearing,
approaching the deep slope overlooking the former valley below.

Clasping her husband's hand, Eliya kissed him, then leaned into him, listening, studying the becalmed ocean vista beneath their hillside.

A late-autumn breeze caressed Eliya's cheek and lifted Danek's dark cloak. Birds flitted about them, clinging to last spring's dried, swaying branches. Eliya caught her breath. "It seems so peaceful."

"Yes. But it's an appalling peace, remembering what Khelqua was."

Unable to say more, she could only nod. Their household surrounded them, joined by the mere handful of Khelqua's somber survivors, rescued from the foothills after the flood. Torena clasped the Rone'en as if it were a child, and Danek's humbly clad religious clerk bowed his head for a simple prayer that would inspire derision in most Chaplet circles.

How ironic that the smallest, most scorned realm of the former empire endured as the only realm still devoted to the Liege and the Rone'en. This, then, was her purpose: to help Khelqua's few survivors, to serve the Walhaisii, and to ensure that her children studied and safeguarded the Eternal's Rone'en for love of their Creator.

Prayers finished, they stood together, staring at the relentless lapping waves far below, the distant tide sweeping in, whispering from the dead waters of a realm swept away.

Vocabulary

✳

IN GENERAL ORDER OF Appearance:
Eliyana El-ee-AN-ah
Eliya El-EE-ah
Khelqua Kell-KWAH
Torena Tore-ENNA
Kiyros KEE-Ros
Cyphar SEE-far
Gueron GYEH-ron
Syvlande SEEV-land
Ceyphraland SEH-fra-land
Belvasae BELL-vas-ay
Trisguard TRICE-guard or TRISS-guard
Ariym ARE-eem
Rodiades RO-dee-Aids
Rone'en RONE-en
Laros Rakiar LAY-rose RAY-kee-are
Iscah ISS-cah
Valo VALL-oh or VALE-oh
Jesca JESS-cah
Danek DANE-ek
Walhaisii Wall-HAY-see
Vaiya VAY-ah
Aretes AH-ree-tees
Aniketos An-ee-KEY-tos
Adalric Ad-AL-rick
Belkrates Bell-CRAY-tees
Belkian Bell-KI-an
Valeria VAL-ere-ee-ah

AUTHOR'S NOTE

✳

WHILE REALM OF THORNS, and its sequel series, Legends of the Forsaken Empire, are written as a standalone series, readers of the Books of the Infinite series will recognize those stories as a *possible* ancient history of the Syvlande Empire and future stories in Legends of the Forsaken Empire.

Why?

Because Books of the Infinite illustrates the building of a fantasy realm's Sacred Word, while the Legends of the Forsaken Empire series portrays the political and spiritual effects the Sacred Word has upon mortals struggling to survive in a fallen world. Think of the Legends of the Forsaken Empire series as a medieval fantasy family saga inspired by Earth's actual history.

History fanatics might recognize a few similarities between the kings of Legends of the Forsaken Empire, and some of our own, more notorious, medieval rulers. Much of this series is grounded in actual medieval accounts and traditions.

Realm of Thorns—set in their world's New Testament era—details the Syvlande Empire's beliefs and links us to Eliya and Valo's descendants in a distant medieval future. I hope you enjoy their family's story!

APPRECIATION!

❋

REALM OF THORNS WOULD have been impossible to imagine and write without my beloved husband Jerry's unfailing support and understanding, as well as editing suggestions.

Also, much appreciation to Jim Hart of Hartline Literary Agency, as well as Elizabeth Kim of Hartline for their extraordinary patience as I wrote Realm of Thorns and the first volume of Legends of the Forsaken Empire.

Special thanks to my parents, Robert and Sharon Barnett for their love and to my aunt and uncle, Jo and Loren Coila for their continued encouragement as I write. Love you all so much!

To Robin and Rebekah Dykema, you two rock, and you make me laugh. Love and hugs!

Special thanks to a new member of my writing team, Sean, my fiercely adorable ten-pound Ratcha pup, who makes sure that I take my much-needed, often-forgotten ten-minute breaks away from the computer for some food and exercise in between lots of quiet naps at my feet. You deserve all the toys and Teeny-Greenies treats forever.

Map layout: R. J. Larson

Map icons: CathyeChild

https://www.deviantart.com/starraven/art/Sketchy-Cartography-Brushes-198264358

Cover art: Shutterstock: Magsi.

CONTACT:

❋

HTTPS://WWW.FACEBOOK.com/RJLarson.Writes/[1]
https://www.facebook.com/kacy.barnettgramckow
https://illuminatingthewordthroughfiction.blogspot.com/
https://gram-co-ink.blogspot.com/

---

1. https://www.facebook.com/RJLarson.Writes/

About the Author

R. J. Larson is the author of numerous devotionals and is suspected of eating chocolate and potato chips for lunch while writing. She lives in Colorado with her husband.

Read more at www.rjlarsonbooks.com.

Manufactured by Amazon.ca
Bolton, ON